WER MEANS *MAN*

Borgo Press Books by MICHAEL R. COLLINGS

WER MEANS *MAN*

AND OTHER TALES OF WONDER AND TERROR

MICHAEL R. COLLINGS

THE BORGO PRESS
MMX

WER MEANS MAN

FIRST EDITION

Published by Wildside Press LLC

www.wildsidebooks.com

ACKNOWLEDGMENTS

Some stories in this collection first appeared in the following:

"*Wer* Means *Man*" and "A Pound of Chocolates on St. Valentine's Day"—in *Transformations* (BuckThorne, 1989); subsequently reprinted in *Dark Transformations: Deadly Visions of Change* (Starmont, 1990; Borgo/Wildside, 2008);

"DeathSong"—in *LDSF 3: Latter-Day Science Fiction,* edited by Benjamin Urrutia (Parables, 1988);

"The Song of the Worm"—in *The Blood Review: The Journal of Horror Criticism,* Vol. 1, No. 3 (April 1990);

"A Midnight Shooting on the Golden State Freeway"—in *2AM* Vol. 4, No. 4 (August 1990); subsequently incorporated into *The House Beyond the Hill* (Borgo/Wildside, 2007).

"Forbidden Fruit," "High Tribunal," "The Grand Experiment," and "Package from Home"—in *Puns Upon a Time* No. 1 (Spring 1982);

"Palimpsest"—in *Procrastinations* 15 (January 1981);

"Root...and Branch"—in *LDSF: Science Fiction by and for Mormons*, edited by Scott Smith (Millennial Publications, 1982).

The remainder appear here for the first time.

CONTENTS

WER MEANS *MAN*

He woke to pain and fear and confusion.

His last Memory was of a place without a scent, a mountain that whispered of strangeness and danger.

He had trekked unfamiliar territory for three days, farther from the Boundaries than he had ever ranged. The air had grown steadily thinner, drier, oppressively drier even at dark, in spite of bitter waters that sometimes oozed over smooth stones and crossed flatlands dotted with hillocks of harsh grasses.

He raised his head and looked around.

He had done the unthinkable. He had transgressed the Boundaries, but there had been no choice. The cry had called to him in his sleep after the last hunt, had driven him from the pack, had haunted him from range to range. Even now, he could sense it faintly ahead.

He began to walk. Slowly, laboriously. His panting spoke not only of fatigue nearing exhaustion but also of high altitudes and fugitive air.

He approached a treeless pass bordered by cliffs that soared into clouds hanging thick and grey.

He stopped. Sniffed.

The hackles on his neck rose. A growl welled from deep in his throat. His fangs glistened in the dim light.

Wrongness throbbed beyond a bush whose naked branches cracked like brittle bones in the wind.

He listened, cocking his ears right, left.

There were no sounds of small scurryings in dry grasses. His breath rasped loudly.

For the first time, he felt fear. Beneath his thick pelt, his skin quivered. He dropped his muzzle, whining like a day-old pup.

And then....something squeezed against his brain, behind his eyes, a pressure that swelled like a pack of packs to seethe in hatred and fear and shift to something new, a cry unlike the echoes he had followed.

He fought against fear and steadied himself to leap. His nose lifted to test the air.

There! The prey flickered, a thin, elongated white flash lit by the rising Small Bright that scuttled low beneath the fringed clouds. Something tall, hideous, just downwind. As he swiveled toward it, the thing disappeared.

In spite of the throbbing pressure behind his eyes, he moved. He concentrated on the scent, on stealth, on the kill. He became the shadow of a shadow, silent and lethal.

He crept forward. And leaped.

The cry sounded again—then a sudden crash of thunder-louder-than-thunder assaulted his ears and fire blossomed through his shoulder.

He spun like lightning, twisting against the flame that spread from his shoulder throughout his body. Beyond his vision, something rushed toward him. He felt the jarring shock of bone against bone. His teeth grasped, ripped. His mouth filled suddenly with a viscous warmth that nauseated and thrilled. The strange cry rose again, twisted with fear and with pain that rocked his mind as the pressure exploded and everything went frighteningly black.

He fell forward against a granite shard that struck his injured shoulder. He spun sideways, and a dead branch caught him under the jaw and flipped him over.

He was already unconscious when he landed in the thorn bush.

* * * * *

He woke to pain and fear and confusion. Without opening his eyes, he sniffed.

His head jerked up.

He was in his own den! He tried to stretch, but winced, then whined in sudden pain. His shoulder burned.

He struggled up, shook himself carefully.

She crouched nearby, eyes staring steadily at him, muzzle resting against the hard-packed earth.

He licked the matted blood on his shoulder and looked back at her.

She seemed satisfied. She loped out of the den, returning almost immediately to drop something in front of him.

It was freshly dead, large and plump. He tore at the warm flesh and swallowed it. It removed the last haunting echoes of the bad taste at the same time it killed the throbbing pain in his gut.

Then he slept.

Two lights later he limped out to the sun-stone. He lay quietly, muzzle on forepaws. He was worried. His Memory—the Memory he and the pack would depend on to find hunting trails in the darkness of snow-time— seemed damaged. He could see everything during his trek, everything up to the moment of the thunder-that- was-not-thunder and the burning in his shoulder, but nothing after that. Until he roused in his own den, there was only a frightening blank. If he should forget other things—the trail to the low grounds, the place of water beneath the high rocks—he and the pack might die.

He closed his eyes. The sun beat down on his spine. There was little pain in his shoulder now, only an occa- sional stiffness and a swelling just above the bone.

* * * * *

He healed. Matted fur closed over the wound, new tissue grew, pain died. He was well except for a small, hard lump near his shoulder, an occasional grating of bone against tender flesh, and an insistent warmth that sometimes spidered out from the lump. He was all right.

But he was troubled. The blanks in his Memory still disturbed him, although less now. There were no new blanks. And he had no trouble remembering during the hunts, following the trails as he had before he traveled into the beyond place.

Twice he hunted with her, away from the pack, testing his skills. They were intact. As soon as he could run without any twitches from the wound, he would resume leadership. Snow-time was many lights away—the air smelled of coolness but not of biting cold. And until then, the darks were wonderful for hunting, as he and she crept among the greenery, sharing warm flesh and hot blood. More than once they lingered in the forests until long after light, spending their energy in mock-battles that merged unnoticed with mating.

* * * * *

He was dozing when the scream shattered the air, startling him from disturbing sleep-shadows. His head jerked up as the scream died.

Then the keening rose.

He leaped...and nearly fell when his shoulder buckled under him. The wound was painful again, agonizingly stiff. He limped to the sun-stone and picked his way down the trail and across the meadow toward yearlings and cubs clustered at the edge of the forest.

The scream ripped the air again. Fear and agony and anger twined through the long, harsh cadences. He trembled. He forced himself forward in spite of cutting pain. He bit at his shoulder, as if checking for blood. There was none—only the heady musk of himself and a lingering trace of her and...and a strange, heavy odor that tingled his nostrils and almost made him stumble.

But the keening rose again and the errant scent fled as he nipped his way through clustered yearlings, snapping viciously when one blundered against his shoulder.

Then he stopped.

An old one lay dead.

The muzzle was spotted with foam, the eyes distended as if the old one were still struggling for breath. But the old one was dead.

He looked up, following the trail of ripped branches and torn moss where the old one had fallen down the slope, as if out of a need to die within scent of the pack. The air held an acrid scent, unknown yet hauntingly familiar.

Someone growled. He looked up in time to see her enter the circle. Their eyes met. She backed away, whirled, and ran.

Her cry had awakened him.

By now, other adults were emerging from the trees. He nuzzled the corpse once more. There were bruises, and the old one's pelt was matted with twigs and grass and dirt—but there was no wound that could kill. The only blood was already crusting around a small hole in the old one's forehead.

But such a small wound surely could not kill!

He looked up.

Three yearlings broke from the circle and stepped around him and tugged at the old one's stiffening legs, pulling the body from the pack's grounds.

He watched the body disappear. He felt weak. His

shoulder burned as he limped back to the den, crossing the sun-stone without even thinking once of laying full-length in the warmth and sleeping. Instead, he disappeared into the dark shadows of the den and the waiting coolness.

During the next three lights, three more old ones died. All were light-hunting, even though they might have hunted by dark just as easily. Each had slipped through early mists for private hunting grounds.

All were found with small wounds in their heads and the lingering scent of something acrid and hot surrounding them. He went with the others to see the first one. After that, he refused.

He also refused to eat. And now she was acting strangely as well. She avoided him, bristling when he touched her, so he nipped back in frustration and growled throatily when she entered the den, or snapped when she came too near. On the third light-end since the first old one died, he woke to an empty den. She did not return that dark, or the next.

During the fourth dark after the coming of Death to the pack, he did not sleep. He lay motionless for what seemed a lifetime of breaths. He hurt with a deep, burning pain that was more than pain, that slipped through his body like a fog. When he tried to catch it, to bite and worry it and finally to kill it, he could not find it. Instead, he twisted and whined and twitched with irritation of the pain-not-pain.

Finally he rose and padded from the den, gliding away into shadows. He saw no one, even though the

Small Bright had risen. Clouds covered most of the sky. He threaded through dense undergrowth, pausing once when he thought he heard the faint crackling of steps behind him. He swiveled his head, eyes and ears straining for sounds or movement.

There was nothing.

He continued, weaving through underbrush as silently as a shadow, following a Memory that he could not see, a new Memory that terrified as much as it enticed.

As he went, he felt no fear of the Death that stalked the pack. In fact, he moved with increasing confidence, increasing strength as the pain-not-pain receded and his muscles warmed.

He stopped at the base of a towering black cliff. Again, he had the prickling feeling that someone... *something*...was trailing him in the darkness. He glared over his shoulder, snarling a challenge. Dark swallowed the sound. After a few breaths, he began climbing the rocks, following a faint trail through coarse gravel and littered leaves.

The climb was difficult. His paws slipped on the rocks, once slamming him against the cliff face. But he continued until he reached a ledge mid-way up the cliff face.

From there, he could see the entire valley. He settled his body into a hollow littered with small stones and dead leaves, rested his muzzle on his forepaws, and waited.

None of the pack was ranging during this dark. No

movement disturbed the world below him.

He waited. Finally he slept.

But this sleep brought no rest. His fevered mind whirled so rapidly that the Memory clicked in, engraving sleep-shadows onto his brain. It seemed at first as if the burning had returned to his shoulder, mounting as the waning Small-Bright light bathed the rocks. The burning spread slowly but inexorably until his body was aflame. He tried to whimper, tried to snap at his paw and exchange this phantom, eerily frightening pain for the more understandable pain of warm blood spurting through ripped flesh. But he could not move, could not make a sound.

The rocks beneath him grew icy cold, and the cold pierced his belly and loins and struggled unevenly with the fire.

Finally, as with the snapping of a single branch holding back an avalanche, his head rose until his muzzle pointed directly overhead. The flesh of his throat strained taut and tight. He bayed. The wail echoed peak to peak until it seemed as if a strange pack had surrounded him, creeping nearer and nearer.

His pent-up frustrations released—and with them, surprisingly, his fear—he looked down....

And beheld an alien world.

Shadows deepened until he could see only the blackness of dark webbed by the silver of Small-Bright light on isolated rocks. Everything else disappeared: valley, trees, even the tumble of rocks twenty body-lengths straight below. He could see nothing.

But strangely the blindness was not a thing of fear. He rose. His joints creaked faintly in the silence. As he moved, he could hear the scrape of coarse hair against coarse hair. His breathing became ragged and frighteningly loud.

For a long time, he huddled on his haunches, his rear legs tight against his warmth, his forelegs stiff and straight. The bunched muscles in his haunches quivered, rippled. He felt as if something in him were about to burst.

And then he moved again.

He balanced precariously as his forelegs—still deathly stiff and straight—rose rigidly in front of him and his hind legs suddenly bore his entire weight.

And still he rose, his eyes bulging in terror as his spine crackled and the muscles of hip and knee twisted and his taut forelegs glowed, glistened hideously in the moonlight, whitely smooth and bare.

His claws receded with the whispering of snakes in dead grass. They almost disappeared into long, narrow, soft pads that separated from each other and then wriggled slowly, singly, fluidly, like summer reeds in the riverbeds.

He swayed, caught his balance somehow, then looked down to where his hind paws clutched at the rock.

Swept by a wave of dizziness and nausea at what he saw, he thrust his glance upward and concentrated on the ring of clouds around the Small Bright. He shivered as his lips grew parched. Uneasily, he allowed his body to lean backward until it rested against a rock.

Rough granite dug into his naked back. The rock was cold and sharp.

He looked down again.

His hind legs had lengthened. They ended in useless, flat, gross parodies of paws—hideous lumps like his front paws had become, only longer at the base, with the reed-like extensions shorter and blunter. They had no claws, no hair. The crumbling rock beneath them cut into tender flesh.

And, as if one deformity were not enough, something horrible throbbed awkwardly at the juncture of his legs. It was blunter, longer and thicker than his own, and rose against the shadows cast by moonlight against rock.

His vision blurred again and salt dripped into his mouth. For a moment, he felt numbed, dead. Sight had failed; smell had almost disappeared; taste faded to mere hints of tangy saltiness tantalizing his tongue—*soft, flat, smooth organ rubbing against nubbed teeth that could neither rend nor rip nor tear*—without betraying the secrets of its source.

He swayed, frantically slapping the useless, distorted paws against the granite. A shard sliced flesh, and he saw black blood on the rock—*his blood*—but could not smell it. He touched hand to tongue. The flavor was faint, mild, tepid. A new wave of dizziness slammed against him, and the extensions on his paws flexed like reeds and grasped again at rough places on the cliff. They held him tightly against the coolness of rock.

For a long time, he struggled in himself.

And then....

His head snapped away from the rock and he drew himself erect. The blurring and the dizziness disappeared. Drawing himself taller, he stared into the landscape below. Damp air fingered his nakedness, cooling and refreshing, stimulating his sex as he thought of the night ahead—*the death, the blood, the Power!*—until it grew heavy and pounded in tandem with the beat of his heart. The veins along his throat echoed the pulse. He stepped forward, toes curling tightly around palm-sized rocks. He moved to the cliff and poised on the razor edge and looked down. He listened, but could hear nothing.

Below, in a silvered glade tinged with the first hints of dawn, there was no movement.

They sleep—or, perhaps, not, he thought with a silent laugh. Even though his nose was not as keen as theirs, his eyes as sharp, his ears as keen, he knew they were there. He could feel them—*imagine them*—cowering in reeking dens, dreading his approach.

He laughed, out loud this time. The sound spiraled upward and echoed from the mountains.

When it died, the silence seemed darker, deeper.

His brow wrinkled, and for a moment he felt a wolfish snarl rise, then dissolve in his throat before it reached the broad, flat teeth that blocked his breath.

No matter. He lived and killed and all was as it should be.

His hand rose and touched his shoulder. There was warmth and a swelling just below the roundness of muscle. A small red scar spidered over the flesh. He pressed with one finger and grimaced when the pain flared. *A scratch,* he thought, *infection. It will pass.* And if it did not...well, nothing must hamper his mission.

And so...to work.

This time, he knew at once, the hunt would be different. Each Light before, he had awakened among the enemy to find himself hidden in a fetid hole, ready to creep out, cross the valley, almost blindly ascend the rock-strewn cliff, and pull *it* from its cache deep within the rocks—hidden where claws and paws could never find it but nimble, fragile fingers could uncover it readily. Only then would he descend and follow his chosen prey into the forest, himself no more than a wisp, a phantom, a fragment of dreams too hollow to have form. Twice a bitch had been asleep in the hole where he woke, a ready target had he had *it*; but each time he ignored her for worthier prey and for the sheer, sensual—*even sexual*—thrill of the stalk and the kill through the wilderness night.

But now, tonight...tonight he stood naked (as always) on the cliff, looking down upon the vermin. He imagined dawnlight glinting in open, frightened eyes. Perhaps they could see him as he stood here, erect and powerful, a white glistening against grey rock. If so, they would fear and cower. He breathed heavily as strength surged through him and warmth entered every cell.

A cloud scudded across his mind. He shook his head, trying to penetrate a sudden vagueness. *He* was Death.

He prowled the nameless wastes, sustained by vague, throbbing powers that surged through his body.

He laughed, a nervous sound that swirled and twined with combinations of sounds at once both words and inarticulations of primitive emotions.

He leaped backward, into the darkness, and scrabbled blindly at the cairn of rocks. His fingers ached with the strain as they lifted rocks the size of his own torso. Once, two boulders slid together and pinched the skin of his arm. He cried in pain and held the arm up to the light. The dark patch that was blood startled him more than had the pain.

He turned again to his work. He did not stop until his probing fingers touched coldness and smoothness and hardness. He pulled it out.

It glinted in the moonlight. It felt heavy in his hand, yet oddly comfortable as his fingers caressed the trigger. He raised it arm-high, scarcely noting the twitch in his shoulders, and sighted down the barrel, picking target after target from among the shadows and firing at imaginary prey. Silver eyes glared at him from the roundness beneath the barrel.

He climbed down from the rocks. Once on the forest floor, he ran easily. His body was made for running, for leaping. His arms swung loosely at his side, one hand unclenched and relaxed, the other grasping the weapon. Once his bare foot struck a rock. The pain made him break stride for a moment, then he was himself again. This was what he lived for. This...and killing *them*.

He slowed along the ridge leading into the valley. Here he climbed carefully, since his hands and feet— and other parts as well—were vulnerable to sharp edges. Sliding down one rock face, he tore open the half-clotted cut on his arm. Blood oozed freshly, and he reached over and touched the blood and rubbed thick blood—*his blood*—between his fingers, curiously, as if he had never seen such a thing before. He touched a reddened fingertip to his tongue—*and for a second thirsted for more, for warmth and life and breath.* He swallowed convulsively, his throat long and white in the moon-light. His vision flickered...he stumbled...and then he was himself again, erect, wiping the blood on a rough leaf plucked from a low bush as he ran by. His stomach was knotted.

The soil beneath the ridge grew damp and spongy. The air felt cool. He ran, his mind lingering absently on thoughts of warmth and comfort and thick fur—

On him, not *around* him.

He stumbled, sprawling on the humus. His eyes were closed but his mind hovered madly between two visions (*not true cant be true isnt true*). Then the moment died and he stood in a single fluid thrust, conscious of his pride in the movement as he trans-formed it into a personal gesture of triumph.

He stood erect. Lesser creatures crawled.

He was Death. Lesser creatures died.

Circling a pond overgrown with reeds, he caught a glimpse of a fleeting reflection. Puzzled, suddenly halfway to the border of fear, he stopped and knelt and looked into the black waters.

And saw...a dim white form locked between insubstantial trees. He was reminded of.... Of what? He had never seen a body like this before—(*thin white body twisted bloodily against a thorn bush on a treeless pass, head crushed body crushed flesh crushed blood devoured*)—yet somehow he knew instinctively, as if in a waking dream, that he had.

His stomach wrenched again.

Confused, he cried aloud, an agonized cry devoid of the earlier laughter and confidence. Behind his eyes, two visions flickered, kaleidoscopic and terrifying. The cry receded into tears.

A sound startled him. He whirled to face the forest but could see nothing until a small form—a field mouse? a ground squirrel? as large as a rabbit?—scuttled across the path.

He laughed silently, laughed at his fears.

As if anything could threaten *him*.

He was the power!

He returned to the hunt, moving swiftly but carefully to avoid cuts or scrapes—yet irrationally almost desiring them. Desiring the warmth of blood against his tongue, wrapping his throat with warmth.

He concentrated on the trees, the trail, the sky, and saw no more reflections in the water.

When he reached open ground, he stepped boldly into the dawn, flaunting his posture, reveling in the erect shadow that spread out to his side. This time, he would enter their domain. He would penetrate their lairs and dare the beasts cowering in shadows to attack him.

He strode toward an elevated rock in the center of the clearing. He felt their yellow eyes peering at him from all sides. He threw his head back and laughed—and the eyes blinked out, then slowly reappeared, fearful and wary.

He raised the weapon. There was a long moment of silence, then he suddenly yelled, swinging the weapon over his head, exulting in the words that coursed like sunlight through his body and exploded from his throat.

"Come out! Out of your holes and face me!"

As soon as they passed his lips, the words became crude and harsh, obscene parodies of the sounds that welled within him but still the closest to them that he could create. His throat cracked and his lips burned. Even so, the power of the sounds excited him.

And horrified *them.*

One by one, shadows crept from darker shadows until he stood at the center of a half-circle of huge, cringing, shaggy beasts. The stench was overpowering this close—the wildness, the filth. They approached until they were less than two body lengths away, then they huddled against the ground, their eyes riveted on him.

He swung the weapon again, circled it around his head until the barrel was even with his eyes, then he aimed and fired at a rock across the clearing. The rock shattered with a flash of red. The animals whirled to run, but he cried "Stay!" and they crouched down again, skittish and even more uneasy.

They did not understand words but they responded to the power of voice and will.

He played the barrel along the row of beasts. None moved, save for a silent baring of teeth in fury...or in fear. He raised his arms slowly. The swelling ached, but he ignored it. He gestured to himself, touching his bare chest with the tip of the weapon. It was hot and burned his skin but with a pain that merged with pleasure.

"I am..." he began. "I am *man*.... I...."

He knew what he knew, but the words would not come. He could not articulate his essence. The single *I* extended to become more growl than speech. It spiraled wildly into a cry that was half wolf-howl, half human-exultation.

At the tension in the sound, the ring of beasts edged closer. He threw both arms outward, and the great shaggy creatures shied away from the movement.

"Back!"

They obeyed.

He tried once more to force words out, to make his lips and throat and tongue form the sounds that would fling truth into the air. But behind his eyes, two visions warred, and the sounds refused to accept the discipline of words. He tried to tangle out unspoken, unspeakable Memories, but they swirled into incoherence. He tried to speak. He was the Power. He must kill. Not just wound, but *kill*.

If he only wounded, if the flesh remained alive....

He screamed, a thin, high-pitched cry that hurt their sensitive ears as it careened from rock to rock. The pack leaped back, less from pain than from the terror it embodied.

"I...I...kill! No! *No more!*"

He turned the hot barrel of the weapon until it touched a vein throbbing in his throat. His finger tightened.

For an instant, he was bitterly aware of everything around him: the ring of beasts, the fading moon and rising dawn, cold stone beneath naked feet, rock clattering from the slope behind him.

His finger pressed the trigger.

And a body crashed against him, knocking his aim wild. The weapon flew from his hand and, glinting in the light, smashed against rock. He stumbled sideways, lost his balance, and rolled. He scrabbled frantically for a foothold, a handhold, anything so that he could stand again and fight.

One shuddering vision surfaced completely. He *would* fight. He *would* destroy the beasts.

With a hideous snarl, something struck him from behind. Claws skinned along the ridge of his spine, leaving stipples of hot blood. He twisted, shrieking nonwords as he grabbed coarse fur between his hands and pushed. Teeth ripped along his cheek. Hot, fetid breath nearly suffocated him as he thrust the squirming mass away again, then the teeth were back, on his shoulder this time, gouging out a jagged chunk of flesh where the swelling had been.

The pain spiraled into agony. Flames beyond fire spun through him, and his consciousness splintered into darkness. With a supreme effort, he rose to one knee, then fell, and struck his temple....

* * * * *

Even before he was fully awake, he recognized the faint light. Shadowed light. Coolness. The comfortable moistness of the den. He raised his head and focused. She lay curled across from him, watching him.

His head ached sickly. Inside, he dimly felt a maddening swirl of impossible things—strange bodies, foully shaped and deformed, fragile and unsuited to the wilds. And there was a thing that sent death like thunder. And there was pain.

He tried to follow one of the flickering images but it intersected with the Memory and momentarily blunted it. He backed away. The Memory was all there was. Without it, the pack would die.

After a long time, the patterns settled and his head felt better. He tried to rise. She bared her fangs. He settled back and stared at her. After a time, she relaxed. The sleep-shadows—*dreams* (what was that?)—were gone. He licked the blood-matted pelt around his throbbing shoulder. There was a large wound now, deeper than before. But it smelled clean and wholesome. He tried to move the leg. It was painful but he could move it. There would be a long healing.

He sniffed carefully, then nosed the flesh, mindful of torn tissue. The knot at the center of the wound was gone. The burning and the swelling beneath the skin were gone.

He looked at her and growled hungrily.

She left.

He lay back. Most of the sleep-shadows that hovered on the edges of the Memory had already faded. Many had died. There was something about killing and death. And the shape of a dream-body reflected in a pool.

And something else.

Sounds echoed behind his closed eyes. Some were pack-sounds. But others were more...difficult. Complicated.

Frightening.

He bristled.

Sounds that stood for...that *meant*.

Here was something new.

He growled. It was an odd, low sound unlike any he had ever made before. He tried again, with a slightly different pitch. His muzzle twitched as he struggled to make the sound match one that echoed in his head.

"*Aiiiee.*"

He tried again.

"*Aiii.*"

And again.

"*I* !"

Then he rested. He could teach her. And they could teach the others. And then....

He was tired. He slept.

Around him, through the nameless forest, silence echoed, waiting for the sounds of speech.

DEATHSONG

A month had passed since we filed beside the closed casket, barely able to touch a finger to the polished walnut top. It had looked more like a closed organ console than a final resting place.

And since then, I had not dared come here to play. The organ had belonged to him; we played on sufferance at best, his presence surrounding us as we did our lessons on the ivory keys. Long, thin fingers would stab out, pointing the proper key, touching the correct stop. We loved him...and feared him.

But now I *had* to play again. The janitor had left; the chapel sat empty as I unlocked the organ loft, my key clicking against the lock. I brushed my hand on the light switch; a bare bulb glowed antique gold.

And I played. Softly at first—preludes he had loved, quiet balanced harmonies of flutes whispering in counterpoint. I raised one hand to the upper keyboard and felt gentle tension in two voices sinking deeper and deeper into each other. I almost believed...almost hoped to see a finger reach toward the manuals, toward that single stop that would make my heart cry and wring echoes from the silence.

I don't know how long I played. When I feel like that, I enter the organ, become one with it. Time becomes meaningless. But gradually I noticed that my fingers were stiff, my vision beginning to blur. Each note on the page was preceded by a ghostly presence. I stood and stretched. Outside the window above my shoulder, darkness pressed. A wind must have risen. Something scraped against the roof, murmured against the windows in the chapel.

I sat down again. This time, my melodies rang louder, more stridently as I fought a growing weariness. My fingers stumbled on Beethoven, even on Bach. The scrapings outside seemed louder, more insistent.

And then I knew...somehow I *knew* that I was hearing more than elm branches scratching tiles. I heard something in the chapel—not much...only the faintest suggestion of a sound. But it differed from the others. It sounded like...footsteps, perhaps...or a body sliding across a wooden pew, then lifting itself to stand in the aisle. It sounded...purposeful.

"You idiot," I said, startled as my voice echoed above the organ's softness. "There's nothing there. It's just wind."

But I stopped playing, stopped and stood and peered through the opening between organ loft and chapel.

Some shadowy form huddled against the altar. Even as I watched, it shuffled forward, making a soft scraping as of something barely substantial against the carpet.

I jerked back and my foot slipped onto the bass

pedals. Through the silence rose a muted roll, a deep unwavering note.

The shadow stopped…or at least I thought it did. I sat down, flipping frantically through my music for just the right piece. I threw off the brash diapasons and pulled out flutes, *melodia, dulciana* (named for its sweetness) and began fingering chords and soft arpeggios. In the breaths between chords, I listened. I heard nothing. Even the wind had died.

Then I laughed. What a fool! How many times had I played here at night, with the chapel empty and silent. How many times had I thundered Bach toccatas and rumbled marches. "Don't be silly. There's nothing there."

Even as I spoke, though, I felt it again. A shadow darker than blackness, a coldness spilling from the chapel. And I knew that only music could keep it away. I played, softly meditative pieces to diminish the shadow. My mood altered from sadness and loss into fear; I played the organ—but something was playing *me,* touching stops in me and playing through my soul with deft power.

I threw on louder stops, defying darkness. I pressed the expression pedal, imagining as I did so the louvered doors to the pipe chambers opening wider and wider onto the empty chapel, sounds drowning minute scrapings and scuffings.

I glanced toward the chapel. The splotch of darkness floated down the aisle—a perverse, phantom bridegroom—toward me! sweeping even faster than before.

I stifled a cry and threw off everything except the muted flute and shifted without pause into "Abide With Me." The shadow stopped. But it didn't retreat.

It demanded that I play. Silence drew it closer; strident, vibrant, life-filled music drew it closer. Meditative music stopped it—but nothing drove it back.

The night passed, infinitely slowly. I tired. My fingers slipped. Notes blurred, transformed into disharmony. The shadow would deepen, and I would feel coldness washing my spine. Once I thought I felt fingers on my shoulder, when I fumbled a passage he had drilled me on for hours, I felt the anger.

Finally, I could barely keep awake. The music, the incessant quietness of it, controlled me. I wanted to sleep, *had* to sleep. I dropped my hands.

And the shadow was beside me, blotting out the glowing light, shadowing the keyboard itself. I screamed and crashed fingers onto the manuals, not caring what I played. I grasped the first thing from my memory—the piece we had been polishing the night he died.

With my right hand, I played the intricate sixteenth-note runs, while my left pulled stop after stop, throwing the organ on full, demanding all that it could give. I plunged my left hand through shadows and formed the opening chords of the Widor Toccata. It is fast, loud, exhausting; it makes my fingers ache and my shoulders knot; it stretches my calves to reach the octave-plus chords on the pedals. But it makes me sing.

It grew darker; I could barely see the manuals. I

closed my eyes. The cold swirled closer, joining sounds like branches scraping—but inside my head, painful and insistent.

"Damn you!" I screamed, as I thrust out my foot to begin the melody. "Damn you! Leave me alone!"

My toe touched the lowest *C*—and I almost strangled on the wave of hatred that swept through me. I played, faster and faster until my right hand must have been only a blur—but I didn't open my eyes to see. I pulled out more stops—bass stops, rumbling giants so low I could almost count their vibrations. But I did so instinctively, without opening my eyes. The cold intensified; my fingers were like ice against the keys. I shuddered in spite of my violence as I pressed myself into the keyboard.

And then I recognized the feeling that surrounded me. Not anger. Not hatred.

Envy. Pure, unalloyed envy. It wrapped my fingers, stiffening them to the forward thrust of the music. It pressed into my mind, blurring memory. It wanted me to *stop*. The toccata was life, energy, movement—and it…whatever *it* was…did not want *me* to have that. Power and motion and vitality threatened it.

The shadow spread. Sound and silence, music and shadow struggled, with me at the center, oblivious and uncaring. Only my music mattered.

For the last crescendo I threw on the 32-foot pedal stop. The final chord—ten fingers, both feet, sounds pulling in every voice from the pipes and spanning three octaves lower than the lowest note to three octaves beyond the highest—the final chord chilled with a coldness beyond the frigid envy that filled the loft. I held the notes, pressed fingers into the ivory until they lost color and bleached as white as the keys. I closed my eyes tighter, shivering under vibrations that rattled windows in the chapel. The building itself shook as I pushed, harder and harder, drawing even more from the exhausted organ, from my exhausted mind. One grand, consummate chord to push back darkness.

I fainted.

When I woke, sunlight had broken through the window behind me. I was slumped against the wall. The chapel was grey. There was no lump of blackness at its center.

But there was a sound…a low rumbling, like the life-note that opens *Zarathustra* and *2001.* It entered me, not through my ears but through my back and legs and feet where they touched cold stone walls or wooden bench or pedals. The loft vibrated with it; the chapel echoed it.

I stared. All of the stops had been silenced except the 32-foot bass. Its voice sounded as if from the bowels of the earth, so low as to be barely music. It seemed primal, an earthtone itself.

I straightened and turned off the power. My muscles ached; my fingers, knuckles, legs were stiff and bruised. Even my lungs pained me when I breathed.

But underneath the pain swelled a frantic joy that threatened tears and laughter and exultation. I knew what...*who* I had touched. And I knew what I had to do.

Tonight I will return to the chapel. And tonight, I will play his ghost to rest.

A POUND OF CHOCOLATES
ON ST. VALENTINE'S DAY

1.

Most people don't even know the place exists. The few who do call it Shadow Valley, although the name appears on no maps, on no county or state registers. It is less a town or a village than a ragged patchwork of farmhouses set a quarter-mile or so apart.

It hunkers in a wide valley, ten miles beyond the monument at Point of the Mountains that commemorates the last Indian massacre of white settlers in the state of Idaho. In the spring the valley assumes a green veneer of prettiness that occasionally fools passing motorists. Feathery grey-green poplars skirting irrigation ditches contrast with the variegated greens and golds of corn and wheat and truck gardens. For a short time, the valley can look pretty.

But in January, everything is different.

Winds whistle through Black Willow Canyon— freezing, biting winds straight off the year-round snowcap of Mount Cleveland. They tear through bare upraised arms of emaciated poplars and gnarled, arthritic-looking box elders, and whirl across empty fields scored with skeletal stubble and clots of frozen earth the color of desiccated blood.

When there is snow, the valley attains a starkly forbidding picturesqueness—at the right time of day and from far enough away.

But when Aunt Annie died, the valley hadn't seen that much snow for over twenty years. Old man Willard's four-horse sleigh—large enough to carry fifteen merrymakers through drifts higher than their heads—hadn't moved an inch for three decades. It sat in its own ruts, shrouded in dust and decaying leaves and the acrid whiteness of bird droppings. Its wooden runners had warped away from the rusty pins that should have held them in place.

Travelers mostly don't even know they have been through Shadow Valley until they get to Oakley on the other end of the county road. They swing around Point of the Mountain, past the historical marker telling about the Great Uprising of 1895, then follow the two-lane blacktop into the valley. They might notice the old Tuttle place off to the left, its sod roof crumbling between weathered silvery posts. Or the graveyard perched on the slope like a discolored patch of lichen, faded and barren against the sagebrush. They pass the old abandoned schoolhouse crouching behind its thorny barricade of hip-high weeds. Sometimes they notice Tower Rock thrusting up on the northern crest of the mountains that enclose the valley—most times they don't.

They never notice the old house set way back from

the road at the end of a driveway so overgrown and faded it can't remember when it last felt tire tracks.

That's Aunt Annie's place. Travelers don't know about her. They wouldn't want to.

2.

Aunt Annie wasn't my aunt, not really. A sort of shirt-tail great aunt, actually—my grandmother's half-sister. There wasn't much family left in Shadow Valley when I got the letter about Aunt Annie. Only my cousin Anna, named through some horrible mischance after Aunt Annie.

I didn't make it to the funeral. Only later in the summer, when the searing heat had baked the valley dry, and the air hung heavy over dried-up corn and wheat that looked nearly dead, could I get back to Shadow Valley.

I wish to God now that I hadn't.

Aunt Annie seemed unutterably old when she finally died.

She had lived alone since her mother burned to death in a kitchen fire in 1914. The house, battered by the years of weather and neglect, stood forlornly on one of the original homesteads. Two stories of hand-cut pine Aunt Annie's father had pulled down from Mount Cleveland by horse team to build a home for his wives.

Yes, wives. Four of them.

But only two in Shadow Valley. The other two lived up north in Canada; they had moved there long before the government in D.C. made it a crime to practice polygamy. Grandma told stories about her father's six-month trips to Aunt Naomi and Aunt Ethel. It was years before I understood what she wasn't coming right out and saying. Grandma wasn't exactly ashamed about her family—she just didn't like to talk about it.

Aunt Annie, now, she was different.

She hated her father and she hated all three of her father's other wives. Her mother had been the last, a young woman, beautiful by all accounts (you can't believe the lithograph of her hanging in its dark oak frame over the fireplace—nobody, it seems, ever walked away from an encounter with a lithographer looking like anything but a sour old witch). Now, to be fair, Great-granddad had tried to do right by all four of his families. The two wives in Canada each had a place of her own on farms separated by a measly little creek that dried up by April of each year. But the houses were separate.

By the time he settled in Shadow Valley, things were different. By then, Great-granddad couldn't quite swing two places. So he compromised, like so many of the old-time polygamists did.

He built two houses under one roof.

The place had two full kitchens; one has long since been turned into a pantry. Upstairs were two sets of bedrooms—six in all, three on each side of a hallway originally partitioned to make the bedrooms seem like two apartments. The partitions came down long ago, too.

And there were two front parlors.

Aunt Mattie, the first wife, insisted on that. The two other wives in Canada were all right with her, she is supposed to have said when Great-granddad began roughing out plans for the house on the Shadow Valley homestead, but no other woman would ever tell her what to do in her own parlor. So even before Aunt Annie's mother officially became part of the family, Great-granddad built the house with two parlors on the ground floor.

Aunt Mattie filled up her allotment of bedrooms easily—my grandma and her two sisters in one, four brothers in the other. Mattie's side of the house was lively, if Grandma's stories can be trusted.

The other side was much, much quieter.

There was only one child. Annie. There had been others, but they were all born dead—one stillborn, one with the umbilical cord cinched so tightly around his neck that it nearly cut through the tender flesh. Family gossip, not yet stilled by the passing years, also whispered of hideous deformities.

At any rate, there was "Aunt" Rachel, alone in spite of the growing crowds around her. I remember Grandma telling me about Rachel sitting hour after hour in her parlor, Annie playing quietly with a box of old buttons and a needle and a string with no knot at the end—it curled like a snake back into the button box, and almost as quickly as the large, hand-carved buttons slipped onto her string they fell again into the pile at the bottom of the box. Annie never seemed to notice that she was making no progress at all.

Rachel hated everything about her life. Everything except Annie. The baby received all of the love the woman had to offer. Maybe too much of it.

And Rachel always complained, mostly about not having things. By the time Grandma could remember clearly (she was Mattie's youngest, born in 1895, about three years after Rachel finally delivered a living child), Great-granddad was having a rough time. He had to quit his trips to Canada. He had no money for them any more, and besides, the kids up there were almost fully grown. He sold both farmhouses eventually. I don't know what happened to the wives and kids.

But with eight youngsters still in Shadow Valley, he was pressed to find the wherewithal to care for them. Grandma told stories of sparse winters and cold nights when the three girls would huddle together beneath a single worn quilt. Their teeth would chatter as loudly as the wind and screaming snow outside.

Aunt Rachel, of course, had only one child to care for, so she got less than Aunt Mattie—much less than she felt she deserved. She had her parlor, her kitchen, her suite of empty bedrooms so cold that beards of ice caked the windows in the dead of winter. Two of the rooms were vacant, since Annie always slept in her mother's bed. Mattie envied those two empty rooms whenever she saw her four boys cramped into a room barely large enough for two, but she never mentioned them to Rachel. Rachel guarded the rooms with the acquisitiveness a dragon feels for its hoard.

But Rachel believed to the bottom of her heart that

she deserved more.

She took her bitterness out on the others. Great-granddad died in 1910 when a horse-drawn plow skittered over the frozen earth one day in early spring and sliced him open from throat to groin. Rachel had warned him that the ground was too hard. As he stomped out the kitchen door, she stared at him with an expression the rest of the family grew to understand, to hate...and to fear. She had warned him but he wouldn't listen.

Over the years she warned others as well, about many things. The lucky ones listened.

Edmond went next, less than a month after his father's burial. In those years before inoculations and adequate medical treatment, *diphtheria* was a word that struck dread into every mother's heart. Grandma told me once about watching her brother choke to death on a cot in the kitchen, his face twisted in agony, his throat grey and dead-looking even before the last of life left his body. Rachel had warned him about going fishing with Joe Miller, the neighbor boy who showed the first signs of the disease the night they came home with the first catch of the year. Joe Miller was dead three days later. Edmond lasted a week.

And then he was dead, too.

Albert went that summer. At twenty-two he suddenly had to assume the mantle of eldest son and man of the house. He took his responsibilities seriously. One day in early June, he hitched the team to the wagon, sharpened his axe, and headed into the ranges below Mount

Cleveland to cut wood for winter. Rachel warned him not to go alone. She warned him about rattlers and rocky trails and trees that fell the wrong way and sharp axes that sometimes willfully severed human flesh instead of timber.

She warned him.

The team returned just after supper that night. The buck wagon was half full of cut ash—it made the hottest fires, Albert knew. The search parties didn't find Albert's crushed remains for a week; by that time, there was little left of his face and hands and feet, and the flesh along his rib cage had been ripped off in ragged strips—but there was enough left to see the hideous gash that had nearly severed his right leg, and the blood-stained axe lying next to the body in a pool of crusted brown that was Albert's blood.

Rachel nodded once when she heard the news. She had warned him.

Aunt Mattie was pretty old by that time, a good twenty years older than Rachel. For a while, she tried to keep the farm going, but she didn't have the heart for it. Finally, she just picked up and left. She moved herself and what was left of her family down the road to Oakley where she had folks. Somehow, Rachel found the money to buy the place from Mattie—money from her family maybe, although no one knew where she came from or who her folks were. The money was there, though, right to the dollar to meet the price Mattie had put on the house, the farm, the animals. Rachel paid, and Mattie left.

None of Mattie's kids came back to Shadow Valley except Grandma, when she got married.

The move left Rachel alone with the house...and with Annie.

She locked up most of the rooms the way they were on the day Mattie left. No one I know ever went into the bedrooms on Mattie's side of the house until the day Aunt Annie died. Rachel used Mattie's parlor. Oh yes, she moved her heavy Victorian plush couch in front of the west window (she had always coveted that window) and spent hours watching the sunsets in the summer. She re-arranged her furniture throughout the ground floor; she even sent away to Chicago and New York for new pieces, things that Great-Grandpa had not allowed her to buy.

I suppose she was finally happy.

And every February 14th, the postman hand delivered a one-pound box of chocolates.

At first they came by special carriage from Burlington, the nearest town of any size. Most of the people in Shadow Valley figured that Rachel sent them herself. After what she considered years of neglect, she must have needed something tangible to prove something to her self—so every February 14th there came a gaudy box, stiff with ribbons and satin and filled with chocolates. She let everyone she spoke to know about the chocolates, but no one ever tasted any. Unless it was Annie.

Rachel and Annie lived together for a few years, both of them increasingly reclusive—just the aging woman and a pretty young thing, slender as a willow. At first there was a good deal of sympathy for the two women, isolated and alone. But sympathy was rapidly replaced by caution, and caution by avoidance.

There was something wrong at Aunt Annie's place.

It took a while for the rest of Shadow Valley to notice, but there was definitely something wrong.

First off, the animals died.

Not of a sudden, nothing like that. Maybe even some of them just wandered off. Probably the wolves that still haunted the lower mountains got a few that first winter.

But when Old Man Willard drove out in the spring of 1911, there wasn't any stock at all. He puttered around in the barn some, taking his sweet time collecting the odds and ends of ironwork he was buying from Rachel. When he got back to his place that night, he seemed much quieter than usual. Four years later, after he died, his wife first mentioned the dreams that plagued his final years—they had begun the night after that visit. He had never gone out to Rachel's again.

No one ever did.

Well, not quite. After Grandma married and moved back to Shadow Valley, she drove out once or twice to see Rachel. She never went beyond the house but even from there she could tell that the place was going downhill fast—fences falling over, the barn looking like it was ready to collapse with the next winter's snows (even though it stood until 1934, when it burned to the ground), the wagons and harrows and plows rusted, cracking, and useless.

Things like that.

And Rachel had changed, Grandma said. Grandma was well into her seventies when she finally spoke to me about all of this.

"Gone to fat, she was," Grandma said with more than a touch of satisfaction giving her voice a saccharine whining quality so unlike her. "Gone to fatness and softness. Big, too. Big as a house. And her always so proud of her figure. Must've been them chocolates."

"Chocolates?" I remember asking, a boy entranced by a brief vision of a world long dead.

She studied me over the frames of her bifocals. "Chocolates," she repeated, her voice harsh.

I couldn't get any more from her, except that Rachel had become monstrously fat by the time the war came, 1914, the year she reached across the old wood-burner for a pot of oatmeal one morning and dragged her sleeve across the heated surface. The ancient ecru lace she always wore at the cuff flickered into flame, and before she could move an inch toward the bucket of water that was supposed to stand right next to the stove but was unaccountably clear across the kitchen on the counter next to the Hoosier cabinet, she was a screeching pillar of fire, her dress burning off her body in an instant, her flesh sizzling and popping and cracking like the strips of bacon curling in the frying pan not half a foot away.

The floor was a little scorched, but Annie was able to put the fire out with no other damage to the house.

Of course, no one was there to see what really

happened; everyone relied on what Annie could tell them through her tears and her shock. Annie repeated again and again that she had warned her mother about fire. But Rachel just wouldn't listen.

They buried what was left of Rachel three days later in the old church, the hand-cut rock one, not the brick one that went up over its blasted-out remains in 1952. Grandma said that the casket was closed—probably just as well, considering. But some of the folks said that even under the circumstances, it was a mighty small casket for a woman of Rachel's size.

3.

They buried Rachel, and Annie—now a girl of seventeen—went back alone to the old house. To my knowledge, no one ever saw her again, face to face, except Grandma. For some reason that not even Grandma ever understood, she and Annie got along well. Maybe they were close enough in age, maybe Annie was envious of Grandma and her new husband and wanted to experience Grandma's life vicariously through the stories Grandma told. Whatever the reason, Grandma would drive out to the old place every once in a while, whipping the buggy team along with a practiced hand. She always went alone.

They would sit in the west parlor—Mattie's parlor—and talk about this and that, nothing special, then Annie would get a far away look in her eyes and Grandma would hitch herself up and say "Thanks for the nice afternoon, Annie," and leave.

Now, I got most of this from Grandma in the year or two before she died. She wasn't really that sharp any more, of course, and I wouldn't swear by all of what she said, but it's more than anyone else ever knew for sure about Aunt Annie. Until she finally opened up to me, I don't think Grandma had spoken to anyone in Shadow Valley about those drives.

Well, life went on, as it always does. Grandma had children. Some died, two lived—my mother and my Aunt Mae. Grandpa died a lonely death somewhere in the Pacific in 1944; no body was ever returned, so the marble stone in the Shadow Valley graveyard stands sentinel atop an empty casket. My mother died in childbirth. I was born in Shadow Valley, in the old house Grandpa built the first year he was married. Aunt Mae died in 1970, when her only child Anna was only three. Grandma took the little girl in.

For her last few years, Grandma seemed even closer to Annie than before. She drove out at least once a week, until in 1977 she fell and broke her hip getting out of the car after one of the visits. She seemed angry as she slammed the car door and swiveled toward the icy sidewalk. Her foot skidded out from under her and she slammed against her hip. The sound crackled through the brittle-cold air. She was almost ninety at the time. She was strong and feisty, but it took only that one slip to put her out of things for good. She died the next year.

Anna moved in with Grandpa's only surviving nephew—and that's when things started going wrong again.

All we knew of Aunt Annie at the time was that she had become as huge as her mother. Grandma wouldn't say much more—certainly not to outsiders, certainly not to the child, Anna. No one ever went out to Aunt Annie's place, except the Tuttle boy, who left a case of groceries on a wagon (or a sled, if it was winter) that was always just inside the front gate each Monday morning. No one saw Aunt Annie, even though some of us kids took it as a mark of oncoming manhood to stake-out the wagon and watch for her. But something always happened—a sudden storm, a cow bellowing for help in a field across the road, something to draw our attention from the wagon for a second, and then it would be gone. I think I almost saw her once, or her shadow, a great bloated wash of darkness moving through the trees surrounding the house.

Perhaps I only imagined it.

4.

The only time I actually even saw the house itself, the experience ended in tragedy.

It must have been around 1965, when Grandma was still making her weekly trips. I was up for the summer, and my friend Wren and I were sleeping over at his house, about halfway down the road between Grandma's and Aunt Annie's. It was hot and sticky that night, and sleep was long in coming. We talked until late, then decided to play Huckleberry Finn and sneak out for an adventure. Even though his folks were probably fast asleep, he insisted that we climb down the arbor alongside his second-floor window. The thin wooden slats creaked and grumbled with our weight but eventually our feet touched ground. I don't think either of us had any clear ideas about where to go, what to do. We started walking down the moon-drenched road, talking aimlessly in conspiratorial whispers, kicking pebbles with the sides of our sneakers.

"Sure is hot," I said, wiping sweat from my brow even though it had to have been almost midnight.

"Hey," Wren said all of a sudden. "Let's go swimming."

I wasn't sure. It was late and in spite of the bright moonlight, the shadows lurking under the trees were impenetrably dark. The pool water would be dark, too, mysterious with a bottomless blackness that would reflect the night sky. I was enough of a city boy that I wasn't quite sure about a lot of things Wren took for granted, but I couldn't let on to Wren. He and I had palled around every summer since his folks moved to Shadow Valley seven years before, and even though we saw each other only a month or two in a year, he was probably my closest friend.

"Well...okay." It was not a whole-hearted, total commitment, but I figured it would be enough to get me by.

"There's this great place, just over the rise," he said. We walked a bit further.

He cut away from the road and followed a narrow path through a stand of box elders that seemed skeletal and ghostly in the filtered light.

I saw the house first. Its four broken chimneys thrust up like decaying teeth against the moonlit sky.

I swallowed, hard.

"Uh...that's...that's Aunt Annie's place," I said.

"Yeah," Wren said. He was trying to sound nonchalant, but his voice cracked at the last moment, breaking the illusion. "Yeah, so what."

Now you've got to remember that Wren was my friend, that his family had only lived in the valley for few years, buying one of the old pioneer places and turning it into a paying farm. I knew him, and I knew them, and I trusted them. But they weren't family.

I should have said something, God knows I wish to this day that I had. I should have pleaded cowardice, anything to keep from taking another step toward that house, but I didn't. Aunt Annie was Family.

"Well," I began, weakly enough.

"Come on, don't chicken out. It's not like it's a haunted house or anything. We don't even have to get that close to it. There's a pond out behind the shed. You can see it from the top of the hill. The water looks pretty deep. It'll be great."

He took off. I followed.

We skirted the house, all right, getting only close enough to see that the windows were as dark and close and non-reflecting as if they had been draped in death-crepe. There wasn't a suggestion of light anywhere. Even the moon seemed to darken when we stepped out from the protective shadows of the box elders and stood for a moment in the open space between the house and the shed next to the spot where the barn had burned. Then we ducked across what once might have been a lawn and disappeared into shadows again.

I think Wren must have felt something, because as soon as we were hidden behind half a dozen man-sized trunks, he said, "Hey, let's...."

Then he broke off and looked at me. He might have seen the relief that flooded through me at his words, because he seemed to change his mind. His voice took on a new tone and he squared his thin shoulders. "Let's go on. Last one in's a rotten egg."

He ran toward the black, swelling shadow that was the shed and disappeared around the side. I followed more slowly. I couldn't keep from glancing over my shoulder at the dark windows, watching for a flicker of drapery, a hint of match held against the hand-twisted wick of an old-fashioned tallow candle.

I watched, and slowly followed Wren.

And then I heard the sound like a stifled whimper. It was soft, low, agonized, but it seemed to echo and re-echo like a drawn-out death-scream in the absolute silence of the night.

I froze. I wanted to make my legs go on, make them skirt the side of the shed and bear me to whatever had made that sound, but they wouldn't listen to me.

I couldn't move.

A second sound—louder this time, more ponderous and infinitely more threatening—shattered my stasis.

"Wren!" I yelled, and without thinking I careened

around the shed.

Wren was naked. His clothing was scattered in a ragged line from the edge of the shed to the edge of the pond. It looked as if he had toed out of his sneakers (neither of us wore socks that night), then pulled off pants and T-shirt and undershorts on the run and, without pausing to think about how dangerous it might be, dived long and flat into the still black midnight waters of the pond.

Even from a distance, the light was bright enough for me to see that his head was crushed.

He must have struck a rock, then somehow found enough life to crawl out onto the bank and die.

I stood there, staring, numb, watching the moonlight glisten on his blood as it pooled beneath his head and shoulders and sank into the dark soil.

Only later, much later, after I had fallen to my knees and vomited until it felt my guts rip loose; only after I ran home to Grandma's and woke Dad and Grandma with my wild shrieks and heaving, gasping breaths that threatened to become uncontrollable spasms; only after Dad raced out, dressed only in his undershorts, and drove like a madman down the road while I waited in the kitchen with Grandma, my body trembling and threatening to let go of its tenuous grasp on conscious-ness; only when Dad returned far more slowly and walked into the kitchen and dropped heavily into the chair and took the phone from its cradle on the wall and slowly dialed Wren's folk's number—only after all of that did I remember three things.

First, even though the night was so silent that I could hear the *swish swish* of my sneakered feet in the stubbly grass, I hadn't heard Wren dive into the water.

Second, his back and legs were dry when I saw him. The moon had reflected wetly from the blood pulsing from the hideous wound on his head, but not from white skin as dry and pale as ancient parchment.

And third, I had seen something. A huge shadow that disappeared beneath the trees the instant I came around the side of the shed.

That last memory was tenuous, fragmented, and I no sooner touched it than I let it go.

There couldn't have been anything. I must have imagined it in the instant of shock.

No one saw Aunt Annie for the whole time between Dad arriving at the pond and Wren's burial in the graveyard halfway up the hill on the other side of the valley—or, for years afterward, anyone but Grandma. She didn't come out of her house when the county sheriff pulled up in his patrol car and looked at the pond. She didn't answer when he knocked at the door to ask if she had seen or heard anything the night Wren died. She spoke to him later on the telephone from Grandma's kitchen—two hushed minutes of him asking questions, her apparently answering with a curt, whispered "yes" or "no," then him hanging up the phone with an odd look of frustration on his face.

But there never seemed to be any real question that Wren's death was more than a horrible accident. From the bank, in the bright light of day, the sheriff could even see the outline of the rock that must have killed Wren.

So my best friend was buried. Aunt Annie did not attend the funeral. No one expected her to. But when Grandma came back from visiting Annie later the next week, she shooed me outside angrily and wouldn't speak a word to Dad or me until after dinner that night—a dinner that had to have been the worst she ever cooked in her life. The roast was burned, the mashed potatoes thin and sour, the gravy heavy and clotted with lumps of flour. Even then, hours after her return from Aunt Annie's, I saw spots of high color in Grandma's cheeks and flecks of what might have been anger—or a deep, abiding fear—in her eyes.

But that's the past. Wren is only a memory.

My cousin Anna is still here. Now she is the important one.

5.

When Grandma died, like I said before, Anna moved in with Grandpa's only nephew and his family. She was about eleven at the time.

Seven years passed.

I visited only rarely, and then alone. Dad refused to return to the valley after one last trip for Grandma's funeral. Three years later, he died.

That left just Anna and me—all that remained of Grandma's family.

For most of that time, Anna's life passed uneventfully.

She suffered through several schoolgirl crushes. She broke an arm falling out of the oak tree behind the house she was living in.

Then last fall, the dreams began.

She could not exactly remember them, she would explain when Uncle Evan or Aunt Vera would rush to her side and waken her from the dreams that left her screaming, sweating, and panting as raggedly as if she had just run a mile. "I don't know, I don't know," she would repeat over and over, until Vera wanted to shake her out of sheer frustration.

Night after night, the dreams came and Anna would scream, and Evan and Vera would rush to her side.

After a while only Evan came. Vera lost patience with her.

As the nights passed, Anna became listless, not quite sick but certainly not well. She lost weight.

It's hard to believe that now.

Anyway, one night in mid-January, she screamed her way out of the dream again, but this time was different.

"She's dead! She's dead!"

When Evan tried to calm her, she rapidly grew even more hysterical. She wept violently and pulled at her hair as if there were something caught in it.

Finally, though, she was able to talk.

"She's dead, Uncle Evan," she said through harsh gasps.

"Who, honey? Who?"

"Aunt Annie."

"What?"

"She's dead. I know it. We've got to get out there. Now."

She was out of bed before Evan had a chance to argue. He tried to make her lie down again, but she threw a heavy robe over her shoulders and headed for the door.

"I'm going, Uncle Evan. I'll walk if I have to, but I'm going. *Now!*"

When Vera met her in the hall and started to say something, Anna swept past her as if the woman did not exist. Vera stared at Anna, then transferred her stare to Evan as he rushed out of the girls' bedroom—hair still awry from sleep, his feet bare and bluish from the cold—and grabbed Vera's arm and propelled her to the kitchen.

Anna was already bundled up in boots, a heavy knee-length coat, a muffler, and a hat. Her hand was on the doorknob.

"Wait, Anna," Evan said. "We're coming too."

Vera looked at him questioningly, but he said no more. Ten minutes later they were barreling down the snow-dusted road at midnight in Evan's old Chevy, their breath frosting in the cold. Evan was still half numb from being awakened abruptly, Vera was stonily silent, and, huddled tightly in a corner of the back seat, Anna began whimpering like a child.

Evan took the turnoff to Aunt Annie's so fast that the snow tires lost traction and the car skewed sideways, its front fender grazing one of the box elders.

"Evan!" Vera screamed. Anna didn't seem to notice. The whimpering was deeper now, and if Vera and Evan hadn't been so intent on what was happening to the car, they would have felt their blood chill at the sound.

Even when they were safely back on the driveway, they almost didn't make it to the house. The ice-shrouded grass in the middle of the drive had been drifted over with loose snow, and more than once the motor lugged and whined before the bumper finally broke through a ridge of snow and the car lurched forward another few feet.

It took ten minutes more to negotiate the rest of driveway, but they finally made it.

Anna was out of the car before Even killed the engine.

"Anna," he called harshly from the car. "You wait for me!"

Surprisingly, she did. She stood just to the right of the front door, not moving until Evan stumped up the three steps to the porch, followed by Vera.

The front door was unlocked. Evan turned the knob and pushed the splintered pine door open.

Inside, it was pitch black. And it smelled. A musty smell, like a root cellar that hadn't been aired for decades. Underneath the mustiness lay another smell, dark and pungent, that Evan couldn't place but that he didn't like at all.

"Aunt Annie," he called. "It's me. Evan. You awake?" There was no answer.

Evan reached through for the light plate he figured

must be next to the door. His hand slid up and down the wall for a long time, his fingers searching for the switch.

"Damn, where's the light," he mumbled.

"She doesn't have electricity," Anna murmured back. "Remember?" He stared at the girl, then spoke to Vera.

"Bring me the flashlight from the glove compartment." Vera started to say something, then thought better of it and tramped back through the snow to the car. They could hear the *click click click* as the hot engine cooled rapidly.

"You two go back to the car and wait there," Evan said to Anna when Vera handed him the flash.

"No," Anna said. "I can't. I've got to go in with you." He looked at her, shrugged, and turned on the flashlight, aiming it into the dark interior of the house. Something scuttled across the carpet and disappeared into the blackness at the end of the entry hall. Evan stepped in. Anna followed, then Vera.

The doors on the right—the ones that led to Rachel's old parlor—were closed tightly. But the ones on the left were open an inch or two. Evan pulled on one and shivered as the old wood slid away, baring a deep pit of blackness. He flashed the light inside.

Whenever Rachel's daughter had died, it was recent.

The body wasn't discolored, hadn't started to decay. Aunt Annie sat on the old Victorian sofa, her body so huge that it hardly seemed possible for the couch to support her dead weight. She was swathed in the remains of some ancient gown that hung in grey folds over her body.

She seemed peaceful.

Anna walked past Evan. The flashlight caught her outline and flung it onto the wall opposite. The shadow danced and jittered as Evan's hand shook—from cold as much as from shock—until it seemed possessed, demonic.

Anna laid the back of her hand on Aunt Annie's cheek. "It's cold. Like ice."

Evan approached her and drew her away from the body. "Come on, we've got to get home. We'll call from there."

"Call?"

"Hospital in Burlington. Sheriff. The mortuary. Whoever." When they left, they carefully closed the door to the parlor. Aunt Annie rested for the last time on the sofa in Mattie's parlor, beneath the western window.

6.

The next day, an hour or so after the hearse from the Quint Mortuary in Burlington (who had buried Shadow Valley's dead for thirty years) removed the body, Vera came with a couple of other older women who had spent their adult lives wondering about Aunt Annie and her house and what might lie inside.

They were going to "take care of things," now that Aunt Annie was finally gone.

For the second time in two days, for only the second

time since 1914, someone other than Rachel, Annie, or Grandma entered the house.

The women pushed through the open doors of Mattie's parlor first. The room was immaculate. Whatever else Annie had become in her old age, no one could fault her housekeeping. There was not a speck of dust, not a whisper of dirt. The room was like a museum showpiece. Even the ninety-year old wooden legs of the ornately carved Victorian sofa—now bereft of their weighty burden—gleamed softly in the filtered light.

The doors opposite, opening into what had been Rachel's parlor, were closed and locked. Vera tugged at the knob once or twice and thought she felt the old mechanism inside give, but by unspoken consensus the women filed down the hallway instead and disappeared into the rear of the house.

The kitchen was as sterile as the rest of the house. The table and counters were starkly bare, gleaming in the bright sunlight that cut through clean windows. The cupboard doors were closed tightly. When Vera and the others opened them, they discovered only half a box of crackers tucked in one corner of the far cupboard. In the smaller one to the right of the sink they found a single chipped plate and one ceramic mug.

The drawers were empty as well, except for one table knife, one fork, and one spoon in the silverware drawer. In the next drawer over, they found a long, sharp bread knife and a spoon large enough to serve as a ladle.

Two pots—scrubbed inside and out—sat on the rear of the antique wood-burning stove that had survived the inferno that Rachel had become and had still served her daughter almost three quarters of a century later.

Other than the box of crackers, there was no food in the kitchen. And none in the pantry across the hall either, in what had once been Rachel's kitchen.

One bedroom upstairs had been used. The mattress sagged where Annie's bulk had lain on it for so many years. A single wardrobe held two ragged dresses. Two hand-stitched quilts, so old that the material in the patchwork double-wedding-ring tops had faded to a uniform ecru, lay folded at the foot of the bed. There was no mirror, nothing on the wall except three old prints, unrecognizable faces so washed out by time that they seemed more ghostly memories than pictures.

The other bedrooms were empty. The doors were closed but unlocked. Inside, there was nothing. No carpets, no beds, no wardrobes, no paper on the splintered wood walls.

Nothing.

That left only one room to explore. Rachel's parlor. Standing before the locked sliding doors, Vera felt a moment's pang. She wasn't sure whether they should try to force it or wait for later, but old Mrs. Hodgfield shouldered past her. Now that Annie was gone, Myrtle Hodgfield was oldest inhabitant of the valley and as stubborn as the mules her husband bred until one kicked him in the head in 1929 and sent him spinning into a better world. With a *humph* she took a knob in each hand and yanked.

The lock gave way so abruptly that Myrtle Hodgfield almost tumbled into the room. The other women were pressing close behind her, Vera leading the pack.

Halfway open, the doors shuddered to a halt. The wood creaked and groaned but the women grabbed the doors and pulled. Whatever had obstructed the doors gave way and the heavy panel slid the rest of the way into the walls with a rustled whispering like dry winter snow.

The women entered Rachel's parlor. It stank.

The walls were hung with peeling wallpaper in a design not made since the turn of the century. The floor was so littered with papers that none of the women could tell if there was hardwood beneath or carpeting. They could see yellowed newspapers, old circulars advertising products that disappeared before the second World War, crumpled Grange bulletins announcing meetings scheduled for sometime in 1939.

Myrtle Hodgfield took a step toward the center of the room. Beneath the papers stacked up along the wall, something scuttled away.

Myrtle Hodgfield shrieked and jerked back. Her scream—and the sudden backward pressure of her bulk—forced the others to retreat suddenly into the hall.

Vera muttered under her breath something that might have been, "Lived on a farm for seventy-eight years and scared of a rat!" had she not been afraid of what Myrtle Hodgfield would say if she had heard. Instead,

Vera contented herself with mumbling and stalked into the room, her pride and dignity dented both by Myrtle's preceding her there and because one of the women had stepped on her toe as well. Vera walked across the papers—gingerly, to be sure—threading her way between tottering stacks, and stopped at the dark oak highboy against the far wall.

It was piled with boxes.

Boxes gaudy with satin and ribbon, reeking of rotting paper and old glue and something else, heavy and cloying.

Vera opened one.

Chocolates. The whole box was full of chocolates, with only one piece missing.

She opened another box. One piece missing.

She began tossing covers right and left, pawing through the stacks of boxes.

Chocolates, all of them missing a single piece.

She noticed what looked like tiny teeth marks scratched across some—mice, she thought, and shuddered at the thought of vermin running freely across a parlor highboy. But most of the candies were untouched even though they had turned chalky with age and some were dried and crumbling into the boxes.

She turned and stared at the other women.

Then she turned back and began counting the boxes, one by one. There were seventy gaudy Valentine's Day boxes. And seventy pieces of chocolate missing. No more. No less.

Underneath the candy boxes lay other boxes, filled

with old photographs and prints, most of them prob-ably family portraits although no one present could identify any of the faces. The women gingerly carried the boxes of picture out to the backyard and burned them in the incinerator. But Vera stacked the boxes of chocolate neatly in one comer.

Later, when asked why she had done something so obviously odd, Vera couldn't explain.

7.

Aunt Annie stayed in the Burlington mortuary for two days.

Evan arranged to have the body returned to Shadow Valley on the afternoon before the funeral and set up in Mattie's parlor. It wasn't much of a viewing by Shadow Valley standards but a few people came, more out of curiosity than anything else.

Evan was there, of course, with Vera and Anna. Anna said little. She sat on the Victorian sofa beneath the western window and stared, perhaps at the monstrous dark oak coffin on a bier in the middle of the room, perhaps somewhere into her own secret nightmares.

About five o'clock, Evan and Vera decided it was time to go home. Anna asked to wait there for a while. After all, Aunt Annie had been her last remaining rela-tive in Grandma's family (except for me, of course).

They let her.

And they will grieve for that choice forever.

Anna sat there, in the old sofa, while the January night closed in more deeply. She sat, unmoving.

Evening passed into night. About nine o'clock, she stood and crossed the room, perhaps trailing one hand across the polished surface of the closed casket. She opened the doors into the hallway. The icy air billowed around her from the unheated hall. Then she closed the doors behind her, crossed over, and opened the doors into Rachel's parlor.

It was dark inside the room, and bitterly cold, but Anna didn't notice. She walked around the parlor, touching the ragged wallpaper, fingering the hand-made oak mantelpiece meticulously carved decades before by Great-granddad for his youngest wife. The time-faded lithograph of Rachel—young but dour and stem, almost forbidding—glowered from above the fireplace.

The women had cleaned out most of the papers, burning them indiscriminately, but Anna could still see movement along the floorboards as mice—no, she decided, as *rats* scuttled about, searching vainly for their old hiding places. In spite of the comings and goings of the past days, the place smelled musty and dead

Anna walked completely around the room. She studied every details of the wainscoting, every angle and curve of the carvings on the highboy, every polished surface of the heavy oak table in the center of the room.

Then she walked to the far wall. She lifted up the top box of chocolates, crushing a faded satin bow as she tore off the cover. She took a single piece of the candy and, as if not noticing its dusting of white mold or the scratches on its top surface, placed it into her mouth.

She bit down.

The candy tasted...heavy, chalky, dark with secrets. The soft center had crystallized long before and crunched as she chewed. Her throat rasped, suddenly dry and tight, then something in the chocolate registered in her brain and her saliva flowered, swirling around the crumbling stuff, drenching it and making it creamy and rich and thick again.

She heard a noise....

She stopped chewing, the open box hanging at a precipitous angle from her hand.

She listened. Nothing.

She straightened the box just before half a dozen of the pieces threatened to fall out. She took another piece, another, then three at a time, barely stopping to chew or taste, swallowing them as if they were life-giving breath itself.

Without a hint of warning, the double doors into Mattie's parlor slid open. Anna barely noticed until she heard the odd sound again and turned.

The coffin in the center of the room was still closed. But filaments of light floated above it, glimmered in the darkness of Mattie's parlor, then spun through the air, across the hallway, and into Rachel's parlor. Anna watched entranced, a thin dribble of chocolate staining her chin.

The filaments continued to spin into Rachel's parlor.

And now the coffin *was* moving, a faint vibration,

not quite a flutter of the heavy wood, but enough.

Anna opened her mouth to scream. Her teeth were stained brown with melted chocolate.

The filaments swirled faster, stifling her scream as they solidified and swirled into a column, a pillar, a form, vague at first but rapidly taking shape. More and more light filaments sped from the coffin, as if the dead and polished wood were giving up its own essence to create...something else.

Rachel.

She stood imperious, eyes three quarters of a century dead and long since rotted into dust still blazing crimson, lips curled over rotted teeth, one skeletal hand pointing toward Anna.

And then she...it...was Annie, not yet bloated beyond the human. Still slender, beautiful. As she had been just before Rachel's horrible death.

Then it was Rachel again. Annie. Rachel.

Each time it spun through an identity, it became sharper, more explicitly defined. Even through her terror, Anna could see the long, tapered fingernails descending from each fingertip. She could see each hair on the hideous apparition's head as it shifted faster and faster.

Annie. Rachel. Annie Rachel AnnieRachelannie*rachel*....

It moved toward Anna. It reached for her, and the illusion shattered, and Rachel and Aunt Annie dissolved into something else, something hideous, composed of rotting cloth like funeral shrouds, and blood-sodden bones, and black decaying flesh, and teeth like fire-blackened stumps, and *things* that moved in and out, around the bones, beneath the tattered clothing. When something like a rat—but larger, with eyes like embers—crawled out of the mouth and sat perched on the remnants of a jaw, Anna screamed and fell to the floor, senseless.

8.

They found her there at midnight. Evan and Vera came for her, worried when telephone calls to her few friends revealed that she wasn't anywhere else in the valley. They drove out and rushed in through the wide-open doorway, Evan's flashlight flickering like a ghost on the wallpaper of the entry hall.

Anna was sitting stiffly where they had left her, in the Victorian sofa beneath the western window in Mattie's parlor. Everything else was as it had been.

Almost.

Aunt Annie's casket lay open, its rose satin lining a blood-like stain in the brightness.

Her body, thin to the point of emaciation, lay stretched on the oak table in Rachel's parlor.

The withered lips were crusted with something rich and brown and creamy. A rat perched on the body nibbled at the sweetness of the lips.

Vera screamed.

9.

Anna seemed to be in shock but she recovered quickly.

She could remember nothing, she told them after the funeral. She could remember only sitting on Aunt Annie's sofa, thinking. And then she must have slept.

She wasn't surprised when the lawyers from Burlington told her about the will. A rather nice estate, including the house with two parlors and the farm itself, along with a tidy sum of money no one in the valley ever suspected Annie to have saved..

Against the strenuous objections of both Evan and Vera, Anna moved into the house within the month.

That was what finally brought me home again.

Evan and Vera were worried. They hadn't seen Anna at all since the move. It had been four months, and they were now more than worried.

I drove out to Anna's the afternoon I arrived.

Even though there was still no telephone in the house—and still no electricity, for that matter—she knew I was coming. She met me on the porch and invited me in to sit in Mattie's parlor. She looked well enough but had put on weight since I had seen her last—not too much, not yet, but still it was there.

We talked for a while, a desultory conversation that carefully skirted anything important. Then she leaned over and touched my knee.

"We're the last, aren't we. The last of Rachel's line."

"No," I said. "We're not even related to Rachel. She was only Grandma's...."

Anna cut me off with a quick gesture.

"I'm going to live here, you know," she said, with a vehemence that startled me. "I'm going to live here forever, and never want for anything, and have my own parlor."

And then she leaned even closer, her breath hot and fetid in my face, and with a conspiratorial smile that chilled me and sent my head spinning, she told me what had happened on the night she stayed alone with Aunt Annie's body.

When she finished, she sat back, her eyes sparkling with a vicious delight that still haunts me. I stared. It was beyond belief, and yet I believed it.

She shivered once, then shook her head as if to clear it, and then she was Anna again, young and beautiful.

She stood up abruptly.

"Good-bye," she said, holding out her hand in a gesture that struck me as curiously old fashioned. And then I understood that she was saying good-by forever. I would not be welcome in that house again.

"Anna," I began.

"No," She said sharply. "And don't try to talk about what you've heard. We're family, they're outsiders. Family keeps its secrets."

She laughed, a hideous and frightening laugh that seemed to come from a body much larger than hers, much older and more acquainted with evil.

"Of course, even if you did say something," she added, "no one would believe you."

"I…, I…." I couldn't speak.

"Don't try," she said. "I warn you. Believe me. Don't try."

Without another word, I left the parlor.

10.

I've not returned to Shadow Valley. Nor shall I ever.

Nor have I married. I don't intend to take any chances.

One of my children might be a girl, young and slender and bright and beautiful.

And something...*final*...might happen to me and to my wife, and our child would leave our home to live with her only living relative.

In Shadow Valley. With Cousin Anna.

I wouldn't want my daughter to see on her table what I saw on Anna's when I left.

A brand-new box of chocolates, wrapped in an old-fashioned box that was already coated with a thin layer of dust but was still gaudy with satin and ribbons.

It sat open on a table in the parlor. With one piece missing.

THE SONG OF THE WORM

"Danny. Danny! What are you doing?"

"Nothing, Mommy. Just Listening."

Something in the five-year-old voice made Rachel look up from her sink of dishes and out the window to where Danny was half-hidden by the shade of the elm. She watched him for a moment, shrugged, and went back to scrubbing the first of a long line of pots. At least he played quietly out there...gave her a chance to get some work done. She brushed a hank of stringy hair from her eyes and tackled the burned-on grease on the frying pan.

From the shadows, Danny watched her, watched her eyes focus on him, watched her head bow, watched the straight part in her hair. She never asked what he was Listening to. She didn't care. He tried to tell her once, tell her about the sounds, the singing whispers he could hear oh so lightly in the shade beneath the elm. She hadn't listened. She said something about traffic and then turned away gruffly to polish the silver.

Daddy wouldn't listen, either. He always yelled a lot now, about money and things, and usually didn't even come home until just before Danny went to bed.

Sometimes not until after.

And then, when they thought he was asleep, Mommy and Daddy both yelled.

So neither of them heard. But Danny had. He had heard it. It was hard at first, of course, because there really were so many other noises. But he practiced and practiced until he finally figured out which it was... *what* it was.

The Song of the Worm.

The secret melody that spoke to him of even more secret things, deep and dark.

Each afternoon, he listened more carefully, sitting beneath the elm in the loose dirt Daddy had dug up for a garden one Saturday weeks before. As he listened, the Song grew clearer.

Today, he decided, he would reach down and touch it. He would concentrate so hard that nobody—not Mommy or Daddy even—could keep him from hearing the whole Song.

So he reached.

"Danny, what are you doing? Danny?"

Drying her hands on a soiled towel, Rachel stepped to the open doorway.

"*Danny Mahew, you answer...,*" she began, her voice rising to a pitch as she walked toward the shade of the elm.

She never finished. Three yards from her open door she stopped and screamed, a long and tremulous scream full of darkness and terror.

Danny sat beneath the shading canopy of the elm.

His eyes lay empty, as if his soul had poured from them to disappear into nothingness. His mouth hung slack, with baby-drool forming at the corners. His fingers, still short and pudgy with baby fat, crawled through the rich, black soil in the shade of the elm, questing and questing like so many sentient, sightless worms.

A MIDNIGHT SHOOTING ON THE GOLDEN STATE FREEWAY

At first it seemed like just another random shooting on the Southern California freeways—over forty since the middle of June and no end in sight. Not a night had passed during the last week without at least one report of gunfire: a trucker pointing to a shattered front window; a motorist with punctures in the door of his late-model Toyota; a motorcyclist who followed a too-aggressive driver in order to get a license number, only to become a target himself.

Many resulted in injury; a few, in death.

And this one looked like just one more in the series. But it wasn't.

Fred Zimmerman worked until the midnight shift arrived at the Kwik-Time Parcel Service. He didn't mind driving late at night, not even now, with those crazies running around shooting people. He was a safe driver, a cautious driver, never had an accident, not even when he was driving trucks daytime for the company, not even during the Christmas rush, when the trucks were pulling in and out of the yard every five minutes, packed with orders that had to be delivered yesterday.

Through all of that Fred Zimmerman drove calmly and coolly and above all safely. So he wasn't unduly worried when he left the office at 11:43 and pulled out along Third Street. It was only three blocks to the on-ramp, then fifteen miles along the Golden State to home and Thelma and sleep—or, if he was lucky, just sleep.

He drove slowly along Third, watching for greens ready to change to amber, listening to the irritating *ping-ping* that had developed in his six-year-old Volvo over the past three days. Thelma noticed it first and now even Fred Zimmerman knew that there was something wrong. He would have to take it in to Cal on his first day off and have the engine checked over.

He sniffed cautiously. No oily smell, nothing burning.

Just that confounded *ping*.

At the light at the bottom of the on-ramp, he flicked his turn signal on and swung right, noticing how empty the streets seemed that night. Even quieter than usual. Good. Nothing to worry about.

He hit the freeway at precisely the prescribed 55 m.p.h.

It was much hotter up there, a dozen feet or more above the roofs of offices and homes. He rolled up the window, sweat already forming on his lip, and flipped the air conditioner on. He drove in silence. He used to listen to the radio—when he was a kid, he had enjoyed Wolfman Jack on late-night trips—but now he preferred the silence. It helped him concentrate.

So he was concentrating when the Caddy passed him. It wasn't going terribly fast, maybe 65 or so. Just enough to slip into the night without any problem. He noticed the car, though, because it was an old Caddy, one of those late-sixties jobs, with the fins that stuck out to the moon, studded with red lights all along their length.

The car was unusual, being so old, but Fred Zimmerman didn't give it more than a moment's attention.

A couple of other cars passed him as he tooled along at 55 in the middle lane. That was his only major form of social comment. If the law said that he could do 55 in the middle lane, then he would, by gum, and anyone who wanted to break the law could just go around him.

They did. A semi roared by at well over 65, rocking Fred Zimmerman's little Volvo in its wash. He read the name on the side: Safeway. Figures, he thought, they charge enough; have to pay for all the gas they're wasting.

A sedan followed, then a small pickup with a camper shell. Nothing unusual. Just typical late-night traffic on Five. Fred Zimmerman wondered, as he always did, where they could be going at this hour.

Then the Volkswagen approached. It was going more than 65, directly behind him. It made him seem like he was moving in reverse, it came up so fast out of nowhere. It was dark, not black, but deep blue or green, a pregnant bulge in the night. And the dome light was on—he had time to notice that.

That, and the silver crucifix glistening from the rearview mirror. It caught the light from the interior and reflected it as the cross spun and spun, rocked by the vibrations as the VW's engine roared.

"Darned fool," Fred Zimmerman muttered. "Gonna kill someone, probably himself." Still, there had been those shootings. Probably fools like this one. He eased up a touch on his accelerator, dropping behind a bit as the VW rocketed by. He almost saw the driver; he did see a silhouette as the bug swerved around him, taking the right hand lane, the slow lane, since the Nissan pickup was still only a few yards ahead of them in the left-hand fast lane.

They passed beneath an overpass. Another loomed ahead, maybe half a mile, the lights along the pedestrian walk looking like dim yellow beads. The semi was about a quarter of the way there; the Caddy only half way or so.

The VW spurted ahead, and Fred Zimmerman was still close enough to see that it was jockeying for position alongside the Caddy. From where he sat, it looked like the two cars were fender to fender. The brake lights on the bug flicked a couple of times; the driver was apparently slowing.

Then Fred Zimmerman saw a fleck of light and, a few seconds later, heard a backfire. The VW spun away, putting on speed like the devil himself was on its tail.

The Caddy, though. It slewed slowly around, waffling on the pavement before it punched up against the pilings of the overpass, spinning halfway around until its grill faced toward Fred Zimmerman's Volvo, a toothless, mangled grin.

Fred Zimmerman pulled over, right next to a luckily placed emergency phone.

The semi disappeared, along with the Nissan. Either they didn't see what had happened or they didn't want to take any chances on becoming victims themselves. But Fred Zimmerman, cautious though he was, knew his duty as a citizen. He slowed the Volvo and pulled onto the shoulder. He didn't want to approach the Caddy—sometimes wrecks exploded, he knew that from watching the perpetual reruns of *CHiPs*. But he could report it.

Four minutes later he heard a siren and, looking back over the glistening top of his Volvo, he could see the red whirring lights approaching.

Jeff had waited for this night for weeks.

So had Sara—but she would have rather died than let him know. She knew that he wanted to go all the way this time. And she had decided—well, she still wasn't sure, but she was willing for him to at least try. She could always call it off if things got too hot and heavy. She hoped.

And now the two of them were parked at the end of Miller Avenue. It used to continue on, clear across the valley, almost to Santa Monica. But when the freeway came through, decades ago, it was one of the streets that lost out. It didn't merit an overpass, not even a connection with the frontage roads.

Over the years, it had died as businesses moved to more profitable locations. A light or two still glimmered in some buildings, but for the most part Miller was quiet and dark.

Not a traditional Lover's Lane, of course. But it was hard to find any of them in urban L.A., and although Jeff and Sara did not have a particularly early curfew (after all, it *was* midnight), they didn't dare drive all the way up into the hills.

Anyway, Miller Avenue wasn't so bad. The cul-de-sac circled around just above Five, topping a small natural hill that the freeway engineers had decided to leave intact. Through the chain-link fence, the lights of the basin glittered—romantically, it seemed to Sara.

"Nice," she murmured as Jeff reached down and killed the engine. She rolled her window down. Other than the muted roar of traffic on Five, it was quiet outside. She could hear a cricket or two in the bushes that had sprouted along the fence. A bit of breeze fanned through Jeff's old Galaxy, washing away the musty, gassy smell that it always had.

"Yeah," Jeff answered. "I like it here. Been here lots." He hadn't. This was his first time. But Mike, his older brother, had assured him that girls liked experienced men, so he had rehearsed his role carefully.

"This is my first time," Sara said. *She* knew that boys liked to think that women were inexperienced.

"Lights are nice." That was Jeff's contribution.

"Pretty."

There was a long silence. Both of them knew why they were there—and it wasn't to comment on the scenery.

Finally, to Sara's intense relief and even more intense embarrassment, Jeff hitched himself up, stretched, and dropped his arm along the back of the seat.

"Here it comes," Sara thought, quivering with anticipation.

It did. His hand dropped slowly, resting first against her shoulder, then against her arm. His hand was nice—strong and big, but not too big, with wide white nails and tiny hairs along the knuckles that Sara found unbelievably sexy. She glanced at his hand out of the corner of her eye.

Then it moved again. This time lower, just touching the edge of her breast, where her bra cup curved outward. The fingers jerked slightly when they felt the rigid nylon binding.

"Darn," Sara thought, "maybe I shouldn't have worn the thing." Then she flushed in the darkness. Maybe she would let Jeff go all the way tonight, but she'd be darned if she would let him think that she *planned* to.

She shivered.

"Cold?" Jeff asked solicitously, his left hand reaching across the steering wheel for the heater switch.

"No," she said quickly. He dropped his hand. It landed on her knee, where it lay warm and heavy before it began twitching and moving upward, a five-legged crustacean hitching itself up the beach at high tide.

She didn't say anything.

Apparently that was as good as an invitation. Both Jeff's hands suddenly became more insistent, his fingers flexing, digging gently into her flesh, the soft unresisting flesh of her thigh and her breast.

And then she was twisting in her seat toward him, steeling herself to touch him there, not quite knowing what to expect, forewarned only by the pictures Carol had smuggled into the gym locker one day and surreptitiously passed around. Carol hadn't exactly *shown* them to Sara—they weren't in the same circle, after all—but Sara had seen enough to be excited and embarrassed...and a little curious. If it got *that* big, how could guys manage to wear such tight....

The sound of metal crashing against concrete rocked Jeff's Ford. His hands clutched convulsively and Sara yelped in pain.

"Hey," she said angrily.

Then she realized what had happened.

Not fifty yards from them, just at the edge of the overpass for Sunglade Road, a big black car had crashed.

For a moment, they just sat, stunned, Jeff's hands still perilously close to compromising positions, Sara's suspended open above a crotch that was suddenly nowhere near as full as it had seemed a moment before.

"Shit, a wreck," Jeff whispered, awestruck. "Let's see it."

"No, Jeff," Sara pleaded. The magic moment was ruined, she knew that; but she still had little desire to muck around a wrecked car. Somebody might be hurt...

bleeding...dead! "Stay here."

But he was already outside the car, straining to see beyond the link fence.

"Come on," he urged. "Maybe we can help or something."

"Oh, all right," she said, unlocking her door and pushing it open.

By that time, Jeff was over the fence, waiting to help her. "Some date," she thought as she caught her jeans on the top spikes of the link. "I expected something romantic and instead we're going on a hike." Still, Jeff *did* wait for her, and his hands, when he grasped her to help her down from the fence, were strong and masculine. In the reflected light from the freeway—and the wrecked car's headlights—he looked so sexy in his T-shirt and jeans.

Together, they climbed down the embankment toward the pavement.

There seemed to be a lull in traffic. Nothing was coming in any lane, and the only other car in sight was a late-model sedan huddled by the emergency call-phone a few yards away. A mousy little man was already talking into the receiver—presumably reporting what had happened.

"Come on, let's get closer," Jeff said.

But Sara hung back. She didn't know why. Later, when the police asked her about it, she couldn't explain any better than to say she just didn't want to get near the car. The mousy little man, Mr. Zimmerman, said that he was afraid the wreck might explode; Sara didn't even think about that. She only knew that she would rather do *anything* than walk another step toward the impact-starred window staring blindly at her.

Just then, the headlights on the wrecked car went out. "Jeff!" she screamed. He spun back and ran toward her, his own heart thumping in spite of himself. He wanted to be brave, to pull someone from a burning wreck and show Sara what kind of a man he was, but something in her voice startled him, and the startlement transmuted inexplicably into fear...into terror. He grabbed her arms and held on tightly, each pressing against the warmth of the other, closer than they had ever been before, almost as close as they would have been had the night progressed as planned and hoped. But neither felt anything even remotely akin to sexuality or passion.

They were just two just-past-sixteen-year-olds, scared of the dark.

The first police car pulled up within five minutes of the alleged shooting, lights flashing, sirens blaring.

Officer Ron Siegel arrived first. He was visibly relieved when he saw the man standing at the emergency call-box, a white-faced, little man who seemed as afraid of the police car as shaken by the accident. You never knew any more when calls were real and when they were traps and a sniper might be hiding along the pedestrian crosswalk of an overpass. This looked okay. Two kids were standing midway between the call box and the totaled Caddy.

Officer Siegel approached the little man first.

"Your car?" he asked, nodding toward the crumbled fenders of the Cadillac.

"Heavens no," the man answered. "I reported the crash. I'm Fred Zimmerman." He said his name clearly, as if knowing it would make a difference.

By this time the kids had drifted closer. "Theirs, then?" Siegel asked.

"Uh, no, I don't think so," Zimmerman answered. "They came a few minutes later. From up there." He pointed to the embankment. The chain link fence was invisible but Siegel knew it was up there. They had climbed over, then, to get a closer look at the wreck. He would have to talk to them about it later.

"Where's the driver?" he asked.

"Uh...," Fred Zimmerman said. The kids looked down at their feet.

"You mean he's still in there?" Siegel yelled. "Did anyone look...oh, hell."

He raced across the tarmac. The boy followed a few steps behind. The girl hung back, standing a foot or so from Fred Zimmerman, both outlined in the light above the call box.

Siegel cursed himself inwardly for not checking sooner.

If there was an injured man in there and he died, there would be hell to pay for this. The officer couldn't quite explain why he had not done so at once; usually he would have. But there was something....

And it deepened as he drew nearer the long black wreck.

From this angle, it seemed foreshortened, nowhere long enough to be a car, especially not a hulking luxury model. The play of light and shadow made it look like a long, black box, mounted on one end with metal where the smashed grillwork caught the light.

He slowed, then stopped a couple of yards away. Fracture-stars crazed across the front window, hiding the interior in a sheen of reflective silver lines. There was no light inside; no light outside, either. Both head-lights were intact but black.

Unconsciously, Officer Siegel fingered his holster. The boy noticed the action but said nothing. He stepped closer to the policeman, who did not order him away as the boy had half expected. Both seemed relieved to have a human presence near. They approached the car.

From the passenger side, now facing the lanes of the Golden State, the damage seemed less serious. The side windows were unmarked, except for a single star surrounding a small hole in the front passenger window. But otherwise they were opaquely dark, reflecting the freeway lights. It was impossible to see anything inside.

Officer Siegel noted without realizing it that not a car had passed since he had arrived. The Golden State was deadly quiet, quieter than he could ever remember seeing it. Distantly, he heard a siren. Someone else responding to the original call.

He stepped closer and flashed his light through the window.

The glass *was* blackly opaque. It hadn't been a trick

of the light.

Something had coated the inside of the windows, something that swallowed the light.

He swallowed hard and touched the doorknob. It was icy cold.

He pushed his thumb on the old-fashioned stud and jerked the door open, bringing the light up as he did so.

"My God," he breathed.

He turned to warn the kid away but the boy had already seen and was backing along the edge of the tarmac. Suddenly he stumbled up the embankment a few feet and knelt at the base of some dark bush. Siegel could hear the boy throwing up, again and again.

He ran back to the squad car and requested additional backup. By that time, the second car had arrived, pulling in behind Siegel's just as he laid his head on his arms across the night-cool top of the patrol car and breathed deeply.

An hour later, most of the work was done. Traffic was back to normal. Witnesses had given preliminary statements and an officer had escorted the two kids back to their car, then followed them home to assure presumably worried parents that their offspring were safe. Siegel wondered how long it would be before either of them drove out to the point on Miller Avenue at night—alone or together.

Fred Zimmerman had finally gotten into his Volvo and headed home, angling slowly into the lane of traffic, his left turn indicator blinking fervently, even though there was not a car in sight for the length of the freeway.

Half a dozen other officers had searched every off-ramp and access road for a mile around, had scoured the embankment, climbing up with flashlights to check behind shrubbery and brush.

Their reports were all frustratingly identical. No one.

Which meant that if Zimmerman and the kids were to be believed, *no one* had driven the black Cadillac. There was no one in the car. All three swore solemnly that no one had left the car. Zimmerman said that he hadn't turned away for a second, not even when he was talking on the callbox. And the boy, Jeff something, swore that he had the car in sight almost from the moment of the crash.

But there was no driver.

No blood on the tarmac around the car.

No evidence of anyone climbing up over the embankment-except where the kids had come down, and they obviously hadn't passed anyone.

It was a puzzle.

But there was worse to come. Someone from the coroner's office finally arrived to take samples of the red stuff that had spattered over the interior of the windows, the seats, and dashboard.

"Not blood," he had said. "This is only tentative, of course. We'll have to check it out at the office. But this isn't blood. Something like it, close. But not blood."

Forensics found a single slug, flattened against the Caddy's steel interior frame. The investigator figured that it must have been fired from a rifle on the passenger side, from a moving vehicle pacing the Cadillac. He started to dig the slug out.

About that time, Siegel and one other officer first noticed the smell.

It was funny that no one else had. Maybe the excitement, maybe the oily ozone smell that hung over the freeway like a mist. Maybe....

But once Siegel mentioned it, everyone noticed it.

He was the one who pulled the keys from the ignition and walked back to the trunk. There were only two keys on the ring, an anonymous metal ring like those found in every five-and-dime in the country. No evidence there.

As soon as he cracked the trunk lid, he knew that whatever was causing the smell was inside.

They found what the coroner's man identified as human bones. Femurs. A humerus. Tucked up behind the spare tire, half a skull. They were all gnawed, with rancid bits of human flesh hanging from the tendons.

And that was it.

There were no prints anywhere. No plates on the car.

Serial numbers had been filed away, and the Cadillac was, ultimately, untraceable.

None of the witnesses could identify the Volkswagen, or its driver, other than vaguely. It was dark, not black but maybe blue or green or brown. A VW beetle. No idea what year. No idea about the plates, not even if they were California plates.

Nothing.

An absolute dead end.

Later that morning, the final bit of information came in from forensics, equally definitive and equally odd.

The slug from the window-frame—it was made of pure silver.

FORBIDDEN FRUIT

"But, boss! I didn't mean ta...."

"Intentions are immaterial, you fool! How could it have happened?"

"Well, I...."

"Don't you realize what this means? The equations I must re-evaluate? The probabilities I must re-define? This will set me back...months, at least. We can only hope that the time-change will be minor. He had contemplated an Arthuriad, after all, so perhaps the difference won't be too great. And chances are that being blind he won't finish anyway. With any luck, it will be a mere potboiler, with no substantial impact on subsequent cultures. But if it isn't...."

"I know, I know. 'Heads will roll'—mine!"

"Precisely. Yours! But how could you have done such a thing? What were you doing in the lab, anyway?"

"I dunno, really, boss. It just kinda happened. I know the lab's off limits, me bein' only handyman-gard'ner 'n all. But it was so cool and shady in there, I stepped in, just for a minute. I guess I just picked up them time-cubes 'n hefted 'em, like I seen you do, jugglin' like, not knowin' they was set, 'n poof! there I was, standin' in some kinda garden, lookin' down at this old gent sittin' there depressed-like, dressed all in black. You know, old fashioned, say like four, five hundred years ago.

"Right then I knew I was in for it. I'd gone back—and I'd let drop them cubes to boot. But just as I knelt down to pick 'em up from the grass, this old gent leans over kinda friendly 'n asks what I'm doin'."

"You didn't tell him about the time-cubes, for Heaven's sake!"

"No, sir! I'm not that dense. I just called 'em somethin' else, somethin' he'd know 'bout. I didn't want ta upset time 'n interduce any anom...ano...an...."

"Anomalies."

"Yeah."

"Then why the break in temporal patterns? You must have done something to upset them. He was tired and frustrated, enervated by his experiences. He should have died unfulfilled, bitter, virtually unknown. Instead he suddenly began dictating night and day to his daughters, as if a dam holding back the words had burst. I can't understand. There seems to be no logical reason for the time-distortion, yet it undeniably exists.

"You're certain, absolutely certain, that nothing else happened? What did you say to him?"

"Not much, just a few words. Then he stood up 'n kinda thought for a minute 'n said, soft, to himself, 'That's it.'"

" Come on, man. What were your exact words?"

"Well, not knowin' at the time he was blind, thinkin'

he mighta seen them cubes fall, I...well, I just kinda smiled friendly back at him when he asked what I was lookin' for, 'n said th' safest thing I could think of.

"I said, 'Nothin', sir. Justa pair a' dice...lost.'"

PALIMPSEST

3

Call him an ishmael.

Wanderer.

Voyager through the corridors of Time.

Yes, even Time Traveler (for so it was convenient to speak of him).

And now his moment had arrived. The exactly-one-half-millimeter-too-long nickel bar had been remade and reset into the apparatus, His hands were resting on the levers—starting and stopping. And his mind, hesitant to probe too far into the possibilities of futurity, coursed backward, to the beginnings, to the first vague inklings of a machine—

* * * * *

He hadn't expected much when he first saw the scrap of parchment. It was old; that was enough to provoke a certain interest, but beyond that, he was not particularly impressed.

Still, Smitheran was an old friend. They had gone to school together and even yet set aside certain evenings for reminiscing, discussing the latest developments in optics (perhaps, even, one of his own seventeen papers in the *Philosophical Transactions*), or solving the riddles and puzzles that fascinated both of them.

That was probably why Smitheran had brought it to him, instead of to his colleagues at the Sheltonian.

The thing was a palimpsest, centuries old at least, with two distinct layers of writing. Both in Latin, which was rather to be expected. Still Smitheran, himself a Latinist of more than average capabilities, had brought the scrap to him.

"I just can't make sense of it," Smitheran had confessed over brandy that evening. "I can make out the individual letters, most of them at least, underneath the epistle to Charlemagne, but they don't form words. It's like a code, a cipher, although I have never seen anything dating from the Empire that was coded. How the thing had survived this long, I'll never know, but I am frantic to figure out what it says."

"Well, I can give it a try, although we both know the generally sorry shape of my Latin."

"It's not the Latin, it's the code that has me stumped. Give it a go, won't you?"

He had agreed. He took the scrap from its protective envelope, glanced at it cursorily, and laid it to the side of his desk, fully intending to look at it in the morning.

But one thing led to another, as it inevitably does. Finally only a nagging conscience and a hasty note scribbled in Smitheran's unintelligible hieroglyphics stood between himself and freedom, so he attacked the riddle. The later writing—already over a thousand years old, Smitheran had assured him—had been copied and removed at the Sheltonian. The underlying script—what remained of it, at any rate, the hesitant half-ghosts of letters—lay bared, He worked long hours with a strong glass, painstakingly copying the faint shapes as they spidered across the yellowed sheaf. Then he copied his copy, forming the letters more nearly to conform with the modern norm. Then he attacked the puzzle of the cipher itself.

Of course, he didn't work straight through, day on day, hour on hour. He had his own interests, his own studies, his own theories. But suddenly , the letters of the manuscript assumed greater importance to him than he would ever have supposed. For he had the key.

And what it unlocked....

Letter by letter, word by word, he translated. His heart thumped more wildly, his pen shook more visibly. *This was his own theory*! Oh, there were differences; what he referred to as the Geometry of Four Dimensions was here a disquisition on the *five* primal elements; the materials used in the construction certainly would have been somewhat different than what was available to him. But the mind behind the theory, behind the mathematics...why, it could just as well have been his own. Reincarnation? Metempsychosis? The paradox of time-travel made manifest? Was he hearing his own words echoing through the centuries? He did not know. Somehow, he didn't think so, but that made no difference.

Because there in the penultimate decipherable line,

he found it, the missing datum, the single flaw in his own calculations. Without it, all would have been impossible. But with it....

And now the day had come. It was a week since the final gathering in his house at Richmond; tonight at half-past seven, they would arrive again: the Medical Man, the Psychologist, perhaps the Very Young Man, although secretly he doubted that the latter would show (a particular shame; his thin lips curved in a smile as he remembered how very close the Very Young Man had come when, in his juvenile enthusiasm for the possibility of Time travel, he had effused, "One might get one's Greek from the very lips of Homer and Plato." Well, it had not been Greek, it was Latin; and it had not been from Homer and Plato, but he was well satisfied with the authenticity of the message. After all, the apparatus worked. He had proved that last Thursday.)

Grey eyes twinkling with excitement, pale face flushed and vividly alive, he pressed the starting lever.

In his excitement, he totally forgot that he had not yet sent a copy of the transcription to Smitheran. He did not know of Smitheran's sudden illness, nor that the illness was mortal. And within a fortnight, he could not have returned the document, even had he known....

2

The brown-cowled monk shuffled through the corridors, a shadow within deeper shadows. High above, narrow window-slits allowed a hint of morning light to filter down and alleviate the omnipresent gloom.

Mumbling to himself, the monk hurried along.

Father Abbot was at it again, and that meant additional work for all of them, himself included. As if they weren't kept busy enough with requests for Holy Scriptures without having to drop everything at increasingly frequent intervals to prepare Father Abbot's endless epistles. As if any man's mortal words—the Holy Father in Rome, of course, excepted—could ever influence the divinely directed course of human history. As if they could urge nearer that blessed day, so soon to come, when the Savior and Redeemer should call His own unto Himself.

Still, Father Abbot was the abbot, consecrated in his high calling; and the monk only an untaught youth. The sapling planted next to the cottage door at his birth was still smooth and lithe and strong, barely mature. Once a day, as he walked in the gardens, he could catch a glimpse of the tree through a crack in the stone wall surrounding the monastery. It had barely grown to two hand-spans in width in all the years the monk had known. How then could he imagine himself justified to sit in judgment upon the workings of the holy Abbot? *Judge not*, he reminded himself piously.

He hurried slightly, drawing near the end of the long corridor. Father Abbot would be impatient. The news from Rome had been startling...and exciting. The Great Emperor had, with unimaginable effrontery, objected to his crowning at the hands of the third Leo, truly a Lion in the service of the Lord. Well, from what the Father Abbot had said, the man might be an Emperor, but he was decidedly not Roman (this Frankish inter-loper from the North, from that village with the unpro-nounceable name of Aix-la-Chapelle), and he was as yet far from Holy. Even so, the monk sighed, all that Father Abbot's letter of remonstrance would probably accomplish would be more work for the brethren.

He reached the end of the corridor and swung the heavy doors of the library open. The air within was musty with odors of ancient books, parchment and tallow, leather and ink. It was nearly silent, as the monk had anticipated. Only the thin scritching of quill nubs against parchment, like the whisper of vespers floating across a hilltop, murmured through the air. Candles here and there dotted the darkness of the hand-rubbed wood of the shelves, with their heavy tomes ribbed with wood and leather and chained securely to the work desks.

The monk walked solemnly through the room. He paused only once on his way, just long enough to glance quickly over Brother Jerome's shoulder. The old man was the foremost illustrator in the monastery, in spite of his advanced years. Forty next Michaelmas, and with eyes still sharp enough to line the gold-leaf edgings on a Madonna's robes.

This time, he was working on a capital. The thin brush swirled and twisted with divine ease, the monk thought, as an arabesque of crisp crimson edged the ornate *T*. Brother Jerome was famous throughout cisal-pine Europe; perhaps this page—the text already care-fully copied by the other monks—would end up in the private chapel of a duke, a king, perhaps even the Great Emperor himself, or...or perhaps even the Holy Father. Surely it was splendid enough.

Brother Jerome glanced up from his work, catching the young monk's eyes. The old lips crinkled into a half-smile, then the head turned again to the earthly manifestation of the Revelation of Saint John.

The monk moved on. At the end of the library, he drew a large, ornate iron key from the pocket of his robe and inserted it into the lock on the metal-banded door. The hinges creaked with the weight of the wood.

Inside, the air was even mustier than in the common room of the library, although the young monk didn't notice. After all, he was well used to it. He crossed the narrow chamber in two strides, oblivious to the dull gleam of golden and silver vessels stored neatly on the high shelves. Instead, he pulled a heavy oak chest from against the far wall and struggled it into the center of the stone chamber, where a thin shaft of light from the single embrasure fell directly onto the richly carved lid. He wrestled the chest open and propped the lid against the wall.

Inside the coffer, parchment manuscripts lay in total disarray. Some were new, only a generation or two old; others were more ancient than the cathedral in the center of the city, just over the river (its spire could be seen jutting above the gate to the monastery court-yard). Some were centuries old, it was rumored, yet miraculously perfectly useable.

The young monk knelt near the open coffer, his eyes

narrowing in the dim light as he scanned the contents for a sheaf of the proper size and texture. Already, after only a few months in the monastery, he knew what would best please Father Abbot. He reached in and withdrew a single piece of fine parchment. The writing already on it was thick and black, fresh; the youth's as-yet scant Latin allowed him to pick out a word or two. It seemed to be a marriage agreement from...let's see, that would be almost two decades past. The parchment under it was well preserved, of unusually high quality.

No, he finally decided, this is more fit for a page from the Holy Scriptures, carefully delineated by the other monks, then adorned to the greater glory of God by Brother Jerome. The monk slipped the sheaf behind a loose panel in the interior of the coffer, where he would readily find it again, and reached for another scrap.

Hmmm, perhaps this one. He lifted it closer and looked at it. It seemed older than any he had ever seen before. Old and faded. He squinted, holding the parchment at a sharp angle to catch the saffron light filtering through swirling dust motes. The printing was simple, cramped, and absolutely unadorned. There were no spaces between any of the letters, which were so faded as to be nearly illegible, He could identify individual letters, although they were ill-formed and foreign-looking. But he couldn't read the words. Somehow, their meanings eluded him entirely.

But the texture of the parchment was right; the material was pliant and seemed as if it should endure for several centuries more...if there was that much time left to this world. It would serve.

He closed the coffer and slid it back against the wall, left the storage chamber and re-entered the library. In one corner, a well-worn desk stood, empty except for the stub of a candle and a few odd-looking tools. The monk sat down, shifting to find a comfortable position on the hard, backless, short bench that served as a chair. With infinite patience he lifted a thin blade and began working. Someday, perhaps, if he lived long enough, if the Lord in His Wisdom should not favor him with a quick release from this vale of tears, he might be allowed to work on the texts themselves; perhaps, just perhaps, he might even become an illuminator, like Brother Jerome.

But for now, his task was humbler, more befitting his station in life, The monk hunched over his work. Letter by letter, the strange, ancient, incomprehensible forms disappeared as the monk prepared the parchment for the Father Abbot's missive.

1

The sun arched through the open roof of the villa, throwing the inner walls of the atrium into sharp relief. New sculptures lined the walls, the entire Pantheon it seemed, executed by Rome's most outstanding artists. The Venus was particularly engaging, with her arms folded so chastely across her full breasts. The marble had been hand-rubbed to a warm, almost living sheen.

The visitor did not delay long, however, in the atrium

of the old man's villa. He paced somewhat nervously among the gods, his glance returning several times to assess the Venus from various perspectives, before the servant returned to conduct him to the old man's workroom. Soon, he would find out for himself the truth of the matter. The nonsense circulating throughout Rome was damaging to him personally, as well as to the family, since the old man was his father's younger brother. He had to put a stop to the rumors and the laughter.

"Ah, greetings, Nephew Appius. Or should I say *Senator* Appius," the old man wheezed, gesturing negligently at the official trim on the younger man's otherwise spotlessly white toga.

"Enough, Uncle. I come to speak to you on matters of importance to the family, of which I am, as you well know but choose to ignore, now the official head. Since my father's death, I have been hard put to retain the honor and prestige of the family, due partially to his extravagances, due perhaps even more to your own...."

"...*insanity*, perhaps, is the word you seek?" the old man supplied. "Or vagaries, obsessions, derangements?" He laughed, a hoarse crackling whining through thin lips. "Oh, I have heard all of those words. Many times. Many others as well. And from far more intelligent, astute, and perceptive men than yourself, my whelp-Nephew Appius. What have you to add to them this time?"

Appius did not speak immediately. His eyes fluttered about the well-lit chamber Velanius used as a workroom. Scrolls hung half-rolled from the edges of price-less marble tables, more scrolls lay littered in the dark and unforgivably filthy corners of the rooms. A dozen quills lay scattered across the top of a polished length of mahogany which his uncle used as a desk. Appius winced visibly as he noted a blotch of ink drying into the expensive, narrow-grained wood.

At the far end of the room stood the contraption which had generated the latest outburst of ridicule among the patricians of Rome and provided the impetus for this last in a long series of visits by the family head to the old man.

Appius strode over to it, not seeming to notice as his sandaled feet ripped an ancient parchment negli-gently lying on the stone floor. He stopped just short of the thing, stretching his hand out to touch one of the crystal rods set into the silver webbing.

"This is it." The words were a statement, contemp-tuous and absolute, rather than a question.

"Yes," Velanius replied, a hint of pride surfacing through the scratchiness of age. "That is it. My latest... my final machine. The culmination of my studies, my experiments, my life."

Appius slowly circled the hodge-podge of silver, gold, and polished crystal, estimating with his unerring sense for the value of a sestertius how much this latest foolishness had diminished the family treasury. If only there were some way of entailing the old man's assets against his imminent death. How much longer could he last, anyway, and how much treasure had already filtered through his shaking hands?

"And what does it do, if one may ask," Appius said finally, pulling his hand back from the apparatus without quite having touched it. Velanius seemed relieved at the withdrawal.

"Ah, that...that is the great secret, is it not?" Velanius grinned and cackled (senilely, Appius hoped; at least then he would be able to take legal action). "That is what all wish to know, it is not?"

He crossed behind the open webwork of silver and adjusted a polished bronze plate, twisting it to a sharper angle from the horizontal. A sudden beam of sunlight focused on Appius' face. He squinted and averted his eyes.

"Deepest apologies, Nephew," Velanius smirked. "I overestimated the sun's degrees above the horizon." He flicked the edge of the plate with a fingernail, and the beam shifted to hit squarely on a curved piece of translucent crystal embedded near the jointure of three silver rods.

"My source of power," Velanius explained. "I have harnessed Phoebus Apollo to do my bidding."

Appius whirled. "Are you adding charges of blasphemy against the Gods to your debit, Uncle," he demanded harshly. "Is not insanity enough?"

Velanius dropped his hand, suddenly serious, somber.

"There is no blasphemy in truth, Appius. Even one such as you should know that. We should have learned it well from the great minds of the ancients, from

Aristotle, Plato, Socrates, Democritus, from the Greeks and the Medes and the Persians, even from those fanatical Hebrews with their single-sighted monotheism... even there, there is truth."

"And in the Christians?"

"Yes, I suppose even there, although I know little about them."

"You may soon hear more, if conditions in Rome continue as they have. The Emperor...."

"...Will make a fool of himself, as he always does, a tragic, monomaniacal, destructive fool."

Appius scowled. "You could be executed for those words, you realize," he said finally, his words pitched low and threateningly. "I could easily see *you* destroyed."

"That you could." Velanius laughed. "But you won't. At least not until you are certain that you have my properties legally in your name. And besides, if I am condemned as a traitor, my possessions will revert to the Empire, and where will that leave you? Perhaps the suspicion might even spill over onto others 'near and dear' to me." He seemed to enjoy the sulkiness burrowing deeply into Appius' expression. The boy was not really so bad, he admitted willingly, just spoiled and irreverent of age, as so many of his generation were, including that boy-monstrosity sitting on the throne of the Caesars. Baiting him was, to be sure, unworthy and—primarily because of its ease—unfair, but then unfairness to the young was one of the perquisites Velanius had always associated with age.

"But back to my machine." He caressed the flawless surface of one of the silver rods with his wrinkled hands. "What has been rumored of it?"

"Little. Whispers have spread throughout Rome, of course, most likely through the mouths of artisans and tradesmen who supplied the raw materials for that nightmare. A few purport to have seen it, but again, that is probably due only to the looseness of your slaves' lips. No one, I take it, has actually been here?" There seemed more behind the question than Appius wanted to surface just yet.

Velanius nodded knowingly. "No one. In fact, the device is not yet complete. I must make several additional adjustments, and attach this." He held up a saddle-shaped object of russet leather. "Until then, no one is allowed beyond the atrium in this household...my illustrious Nephew the Senator excepted, of course." Velanius bowed deeply—mockingly?—to the younger man.

Appius flushed. His uncle had the irritating habit of knowing precisely what to say to embarrass him, had always had that facility, in fact, since Appius' first memories of him.

"But what is it?" Appius demanded. "Speculations are growing wildly about the madness of the old man in the villa and the purposes for this last...creation. I demand that you tell me."'

"You demand...!" Velanius laughed outright, this time with no hint of age or senility shadowing the sounds. "*You* demand of *me*! I, who have bearded our monster-Emperor in his own den and lived to tell of it. I, who have outlived all of Rome...and may yet outlive you." The laughter continued, much to Appius' mortification. Then suddenly it ceased.

"However, I shall tell you. You, at least, deserve to know."

Velanius walked slowly, hobbling with the pain-filled steps of age, toward the mahogany tabletop, and shuffled through heaps of scrolls, mumbling to himself. Finally, he picked up a thin bundle of parchment and laid it in the center of the desk, pushing others unnoticed off onto the floor. "Come here, Nephew, and look at these."

Appius strode over to stand next to his uncle. Clutched in the old man's hand was a scrap of heavily veined papyrus, broken and worn at the edges, aged to a uniform dusky tan. It was quite ancient, by the looks of it, the ink barely traceable, and the words in a language foreign to Appius.

"One of the secrets of the Ancients," Velanius breathed, with more reverence than Appius had ever heard the old curmudgeon use toward anyone or anything. "An ancient disquisition on Time, Space, and Man...and the interrelationships possible among the three. An Egyptian transcription of an original which predated Babylon. And I possess the only extant copy. I alone can read and understand it." He dropped the fragile sheaf to the desk and tapped the bundle tied with a purple ribbon. "And here are my own researches, stimulated by this ancient knowledge.

Within these fragments of parchment, I have hidden the great Secret, the wonderful Secret. With what I have written down here, and that apparatus"—he pointed to the gleaming web of silver, gold, and crystal now outlined by the afternoon sun—"I have more power than all of the Emperors of Rome, all of the Kings of the world combined. With this, I command Chronos himself, I subjugate Time to my will...."

Appius stared, then burst into loud, piercing laughter, different from that which had thus far punctuated Velanius' remarks. This time, the sound was vicious, biting, triumphant.

"You," he managed to sputter, "you *are* mad, madder than any of the Caesars! Your fear of death has destroyed your mind. You probably believe...."

"No! I do not *believe*, I *know*! With this apparatus I can command a distortion of the four elements through Time. Earth, Air, Fire, Water—all of them, their invisible *atomi*, their grosser compounds—all exist under the control of Time. By means of this apparatus, I can isolate myself from all *five* of the elements; I can move as it were through Time and observe the alterations in the remaining four. I can see...."

"You can dream, hallucinate, invent phantasms. That is all. No one can alter the present to invade either past or future. Only the poets, and even the divine Virgil required the infallible hindsight of millennia to represent the future. No one...."

"I can. I will."

"Never. Come, Uncle. Sit down. I do not like your

color. Perhaps a glass...."

"Out!" Velanius was old, infinitely old from Appius' point of view, but at this moment his voice was rich and commanding. As he had always done—as he would always do, he realized ruefully—Appius obeyed, leaving the old man shaken and alone in the cluttered familiarity of the workshop.

Appius walked quickly back to the atrium, where the old serving woman met him to show him out. As he passed, he noted that the slanting beams of the afternoon sun had diffused among the marble gods, draping the half-hidden breasts of Venus with a particularly tangible gilding of light.

The next morning, Appius returned to the villa on the hill. He was certain that the old man's fit of temper had worn off, that he would have forgotten the outburst of the day before. And besides, Appius still had to make him understand how critical the family's affairs were becoming, how essential it was that he lend his waning reputation to, instead of against, the standing of the family in Imperial Rome. This time, Appius vowed, he would not leave without some sign from the old man that he would make himself more amenable to Appius' desires, that he would cease dabbling in magic and madness as if he were a Greek slave-pedagogue, an Egyptian mystic...or even a benighted Christian.

The old servant met him at the front entrance and led him again to the atrium. Appius immediately sought out Venus, caressed her lovingly with his eyes. The old man might be mad, but he was still a premier judge of art and sculpture. In future generations, perhaps all men would admire the statue he now had to himself. Unless, of course, the old man could strap it to his odd apparatus and whisk it away into the future....

His half-laugh at the old man's delusions was shattered as the servant returned, scuttling wildly, blinded by tears, weeping hideously, her voice edging into a rasping scream.

"Come, young Master, please come quickly!"

"What is it?"

"My master, Velanius, is dying!"

Appius brushed past the woman and ran into the workroom. Velanius lay crumpled against the lower rods of his machine, barely breathing, barely conscious. Between the inert form and the mahogany table, a small pile of black ashes fluttered in the slight breeze coming through the open embrasures. Appius crossed the room in two strides, knelt, and cradled the old man's head in his arms.

"I do love you, you know, Nephew Appius," he murmured, just loud enough to be heard. And amazingly, Appius not only understood but actually believed the old man. And even more amazingly, he realized the depths of his own reciprocal love. They had been of a kind, the two of them, though separated in age by half a century. Both were headstrong, proud, ambitious, abrasive to any and all (including each other) who might intervene between themselves and their chosen goals—Appius', Rome and her destiny; Velanius', knowledge and the destiny it entailed. Alike, and never so close as when estranged by their respective obsessions, their respective strengths.

Appius shifted to make the old man more comfortable. Velanius did not seem able to breathe easily, and his left side lay rigid, stiff and contorted.

From the entrance of the workroom, an eerie voice cried out, piercing the silence which had fallen as Velanius ceased speaking. The old woman had seen her master's affliction: "He has been touched by the Gods! They punish him for striving to be one with them!"

She bit the back of her hand, racing from the chamber as Appius ordered her to seek out the nearest physician. He was alone with his uncle.

"Don't listen to her. The superstitions of the...."

"No, Nephew, she is right. I cannot move. I cannot lift the hand which set that lever in place," he said slowly, painfully, pointing with his eyes to one of the rods. "That is the control lever, and with it...."

His eyes closed, as if in fatigue. Appius saw the thin trickle of tears edge out from under the yellowed lids. The old man was asleep. Perhaps with proper rest....

But Velanius was not asleep. The lids lifted fractionally, and Appius could see the banked fires smoldering in the eyes. Slowly, word by word, with frequent stops and false starts, the old man spoke.

"I have seen. I have molded Chronos to my purposes. I have swum through the currents...of Time."

Appius tried to place his finger on the old man's lips, but Velanius continued. "All of this," he said, "all of this, the knowledge, the wisdom...lost...some forever, irremediably. Lost. And the world darkened, without any hope but one, and that one pagan and unwholesome. I wanted to continue until the end but I could not. I saw too much...my own life...my work...wasted... useless...destroyed by an ignorant boy not one fifth my own age...ignorant...ignorant... fool...."

The lids fluttered, and Velanius was silent.

Dead? Appius wondered. No, there was still a breath, hesitant and weak. He remained kneeling on the cold marble slabs. Somewhere, distantly, he heard a distracting commotion. The old woman dragging in the physician, probably.

Velanius heard it, too. His eyes opened, far more vigorous and alive than Appius would have thought possible.

"Destroy it," he rasped between breaths. "It is too much, too soon. Even I was not ready. I created it, and it destroyed me. Destroy it! Now!"

The final words rose to a piercing half-scream. Velanius struggled with Appius until the younger man finally rose to his feet and faced the apparatus. The sound of footsteps was closer, louder.

"Now! Take that lever, no the next one to it. Yes. Smash the control bar! Smash it, do you hear me. Destroy it!"

Only as Appius raised the silver rod and brought it down with crushing force on the curiously wrought bar did Velanius' voice diminish. Only as the rod and bar met with a resounding crack and the entire configuration of the webwork altered and distorted, did Velanius slump again to the floor.

Appius knelt.

"I burned...notes. No one. ..must....must ever...kno...."

Appius touched the old man's temple. There was no movement.

At the door, the slave had finally arrived with the physician, an unctuous, obese specimen who, wheezing and puffing as he was, seemed in more immediate need of Æsculapian assistance than did the now calm, even serene figure on the floor. Appius moved away from his uncle's corpse.

Three days later, Appius again entered the workroom. The villa had been sold (there was no shortage of buyers; the property was well located and of more than usually splendid architecture). Most of Velanius' personal possessions had been transferred to the family estates just outside Rome. Venus was gone, along with the other gods, and Appius missed her. Only the workroom remained untouched.

He entered, followed by a dozen slaves, each bearing iron-bound wooden trunks. Appius surveyed the clutter. There was little of value here other than the furnishings themselves. He instructed the slaves to stack the now-twisted rods of gold and silver in one of the chests, the scorched crystal inserts in another, the dulled and tarnished bronze plates in yet a third. Others he set to the task of removing the marble tables, the mahogany desk. One youth was already kneeling in the corner, sorting, stacking and re-rolling the tangle of scrolls and placing them carefully in the largest chest.

Appius crossed over to the desk top, motioning two other slaves away. He fingered through the clutter of parchment scattered over the wood. Idly, without particular purpose...until his eyes caught on a scrap. He slid it out from under the remaining pieces, studied it closely for a moment, then began searching more closely through the piles. The papyrus was missing, as was most of the ribbon-bound stack of parchment. The old man had burned them. But somehow this one sheet had survived. Appius fingered it gently. One sheet, a single piece of parchment, expensive, of the highest quality, but covered closely with gibberish (how like my uncle, he thought, first ruefully, then—with considerable surprise—affectionately). The letters inscribed on the sheet were Latin, but they made no sense, Most likely a cipher or a code, Appius decided, carefully rolling the scrap into a tight scroll. One of the slaves approached and put his hand out to take it from his master.

Appius shook his head, gesturing instead for the small silver coffer lying inertly on a shelf. He opened it, thrust the parchment inside, closed the box, and tucked it under his arm.

This will rest with the treasury of my family, he thought. My final tribute to my mad, my obsessed, my beloved Uncle. I will keep it to give to my heir, and he to his. I cannot read it; whatever secrets my uncle strove with his life to hide shall remain hidden. But this shall survive And perhaps, in this way, my uncle will in truth win his final victory over Time.

With a shrug, Appius turned and walked toward the empty atrium.

2

The young monk stretched his shoulders under the coarse weave of his robe. He was finally finished, thanks be to all the Saints, and he was stiff, cold, and tired. His eyes watered redly from the strain of the close work in the dim illumination of a single sputtering candle. He blew the indignant flame out, thrusting his corner of the library into darkness.

He picked up the parchment and rolled it, noting with pleasure as he did so the smooth texture of the material. It might be old, older than he could imagine, but it was surely of excellent manufacture. It would last through a dozen abbots' inefficacious letters to earthly potentates.

Back down the long corridor, now dark except for occasional tallows leaning tiredly in sconces dotting the walls. He turned to the right, followed a second corridor identical to the first, then moved again to the left. He passed a row of doors, each unadorned, simple, with a rude crucifix of wood embedded in the stone near the lintel. Finally he arrived at the last one: the Father Abbot's cell.

The Abbot was a holy man, that no one could dispute. He dressed more simply than the humblest monk of his order, ate more sparingly, fasted more frequently, and lived more austerely. He was courageous—if he included one-half of what the young monk had over-heard into the missive he intended to write, well, if Father Abbot were not protected from secular judgment by his tonsure and clerical garb, his head would probably either swing or roll. And for what? No one would listen to his remonstrances. Most likely the letter would not even get to the Great Emperor. It would probably end up hidden behind other documents, or filed away by a too-politic bishop.

Still, the Father Abbot *would* write.

The young monk knocked lightly on the rough timbers of the door.

The Abbot's cell was sparsely furnished: a straw pallet on the floor, a small desk and chair, the former heaped with volumes of exegesis and doctrine with which the Abbot busied himself hours before dawn broke and after the sun had set. Near the desk, a thick oak candlestick held the last few inches of a candle.

The Abbot was seated at the desk as the monk entered.

"Father Abbot, here is the parchment you requested."

The Abbot took the piece of parchment and inspected it.

"Yes, this is fine," he said, approbation rich in his voice. Too bad, the monk thought; he truly is a wonderful, loving man. Too bad he insists upon destroying himself with these incessant reprimands and exhortations. Especially since they did no good. He could have been a Bishop, an Archbishop, even a Cardinal, perhaps, if only....

"I hoped it would be, father. I chose it particularly."

The Abbot held the parchment up nearer the candle. He studied it carefully, tracing the tip of one long, thin finger along invisible lines. He held the sheet so close that it nearly touched the end of his nose, and his eyes squinted almost painfully.

"The former writing is still somewhat legible, is it not, Brother?"

"Yes, Father Abbot. I tried my best, but the ink had seeped into the.... Should I try again?" He held his hand out to receive the offending sheaf.

"No, this is sufficient. The writing seems strange, does it not?"

"I could not read it, Father, with my small Latin. I know not what it contained."

"Nor do I. But now to work, Thank you, my son. God grant you good rest."

The monk bowed slightly in receipt of the Abbot's blessings. As he walked to the door of the cell, he heard the old man whispering: "May these words bring light to mankind until the end of time."

"Amen," the monk murmured inaudibly.

As he pulled the door to, he heard the quiet, irrevocable scritching of the quill against the newly cleaned surface.

1

Among his papers, his heirs found one strange sheaf of parchment. It was only a few inches wide, perhaps a dozen long, and old. It showed signs of wear along the frayed edged; at some time during the centuries, someone had inadvertently set it too near a flame, and now portions of it were darkened with heat. A few inches along one side, in fact, looked as if they had been charred.

The executor had mentioned this paper particularly. For nearly five years, ever since his disappearance under mysterious circumstances (no one quite believed that Scribbler's account, published as it was under the guise of fiction), the heirs had heard of it; one or two had even seen it, briefly. Now they were finally able to study it closely.

No one touched it; it was obviously far too old and far too fragile to stand up under such treatment. It lay on the green baize blotter, a tiny remnant of Antiquity which had survived into the present, beyond even into the triumphant reign of the great Victoria.

They studied it closely. Among the many unknowns surrounding his disappearance, this manuscript was perhaps the most closely concealed in darkness. As they looked, three things caught their attention. First, and most difficult to see, they noted the narrow rows of ragged bits of letters which criss-crossed the entire artifact. The ink had been largely removed, either purposefully centuries before, or accidentally, through the irresistible abrasion of time. Leaning over the blotter, one of the great-uncles, a rather fragile-looking specimen of scholarly type, examined the minute indentations carefully with a hand-glass. He remained immobile for some minutes before slowly regaining an erect position and announcing:

"Latin, by Jove, and deucedly old. Augustan, I would say, at the least. Perhaps a few decades older. Some sort of cryptogram, though. Can't make out a word of it."

The other heirs nodded sagely and silently.

They let that mystery rest.

The second matter of interest involved more letters on the parchment. These too were present only negatively, carefully cleaned splotches larger, more widely spaced than the first. And there was no question but that the ink had been removed recently. The shapes of the letters were highlighted, clean against the dusky, worn surface of the rest of the parchment.

Again the scholar made his pronouncement.

"Mid-ninth century, I would say. Latin again, ecclesiastical, although curiously unlearned. Addressed to Charlemagne, as nearly as I can make out, sometime after the Coronation. No signature. No date. Nothing to fix it any closer. Some antiquarian value, but little else, a few pounds perhaps."

Again he struggled to the ramrod stiffness of his earlier days and surveyed the assembly of heirs. A maiden aunt nodded her behatted head slowly as if to indicate that she had always suspected as much,

The third mystery was simultaneously more obvious and more obscure than the first two. No one needed a hand-glass to discover it, no one needed a scholarly background in dead languages to decipher it; yet none present understood it or could even begin to.

Scrawled across the sheet, in modern script, in modern ink, presumably with a modern nub, was a single word, undoubtedly in the long-departed's own spidery handwriting, but totally meaningless: "Weena."

In the end, the scholarly grand-uncle received legal possession of the fragmentary manuscript. He placed it carefully in a thin metal box he had had prepared for the artifact. When he arrived home that evening, he took it immediately up to his library,

He was proud of that library, an antiquarian's delight. The walls were bookshelves from floor to ceiling, stuffed with all imaginable sorts and sizes of volumes, The air was redolent with dust and leather and age, golden in the glow of the rose-shaded lamp sitting on the high-topped desk. The room was perhaps too full of artifacts, but the old gentleman felt very much at home in the clutter; after all, it had taken him a lifetime to accumulate it. Indeed, he often boasted (laughingly, but with more than a measure of truth) that there were items in that library which *he* no longer recognized, which could remain incognito upon the shelves forever unless someone eventually should ever bother to catalogue the collection.

He crossed over to the north wall, separated two volumes and slid the thin box between them. Standing back a pace or two, he surveyed the results.

"There," he muttered to himself, "that should keep Mrs. Princhard from 'dusting' the manuscript until I have finished dinner. When will that woman learn to stay out of my library. That infernal, interminable dusting!"

The old gentleman shuffled out of the library, carefully securing the latch behind him. He began the long descent of the staircase leading to the first floor and the dining room. Halfway down, he stopped, surprised at the odd fluttering in his chest.

"Nerves," he assured himself. "Just nerves. Trying day. Can't wait to get to work on that palimpsest. Just dinner first, then a spot of brandy. Maybe a short nap. A short nap."

* * * * *

They might well have listened with greater attention to the words of the Scribbler:

> One cannot choose but wonder. Will he ever return? It may be that he swept back into the past, and fell among the blood-drinking, hairy savages of the Age of Unpolished Stone.... Or did he go forward, into one of the nearer ages, in which men are still men, but with the riddles of our own time answered and its wearisome problems solved?

Perhaps not so far back—perhaps only to a sunlit workroom in an outlying structure of a city draped in Imperial Tyrian, or to a musty cell cloistered from a world increasingly confused, disturbed, secular—caught in the unalterable consequences of his own discoveries. "One cannot choose but wonder."

For he was the voyager.
Wanderer through Time.
Call him an ishmael.

HIGH TRIBUNAL

Admiral O. W. Homes scowled and sighed.

Why me? he thought crossly. Someone had to be the first to establish new legal precedents under the revised service regs, of course; *but why me?* He had advised against the revisions—strenuously, in fact; but his advice had been ignored. And now he was adjudicating the first case. Captain Bryant had made certain threats concerning Enlist Brown's recreational activities. Brown had continued said activities. Bryant had enforced his threats...and Brown had filed suit against his commanding officer on the newly defined charge of Infringement of Personal Dignity. An enlisted man, bringing his commander officer up on charges! Where was discipline, the *esprit de corps?*

He sighed again as he reviewed the testimony.

Brown's hobby had in no way interfered with his duties aboard the Space Arm vessel *Andromeda*—even Captain Bryant admitted to that during his defense testimony. Yet Bryant had insisted upon the degrading punishment, in contravention to all common procedure. The fool. His own men were forced to bear witness against him. Homes reviewed the salient points:

"Quartermaster J. F. Cooper, you were ordered to issue a uniform made according to Captain Bryant's express specifications. It was to be constructed of vegetable fibers, colored with archaic chemical dyes (possibly carcinogenic), clumsily stitched by hand according to a pattern obsolete in the Navy for three hundred years. Is that correct?"

"Yes, sir. And the uniform was to be three sizes too large. "

"Three sizes? Would you consider such an order unusual?"

"Very unusual, sir."

"Armorer C. Brocton, you were to provide an instrument of old-fashioned steel. The blade was to be six centimeters long, dull on both outside edges, with a five centimeter slit hollowed along the middle of the blade. The inner edges were to be honed for cutting. The blade was to be slightly concave. Is this correct?"

"Yes, sir."

"Is this the instrument?"

"Yes, sir."

"Do you consider such an instrument unusual?"

"Yes, sir. In this age of force-blades and lasers, very unusual."

"Galley Chief W. Irving, you put in at Colony E-52 and while there took on board 100 kilos of a raw tuber originally indigenous to Terra. In light of the synthos aboard the *Andromeda*, such tubers would be grossly inefficient as food, wasteful of space, and thus highly unusual to take on board. Am I correct?"

"Yes, sir. Highly unusual."

Homes sat back and surveyed the court-martial chamber. Bryant was flushed and angry; Brown, thin and unassuming. Not one to cause trouble, on first glance, but then, one never knew. Homes brushed a pair of switches. The wall behind the rows of witnesses and spectators glowed with holograms.

One was of Brown's hobby—and thus of the source of today's action. The holos showed Brown's needle-work: embroidery, tatting, bargello, needlepoint—but mostly crewel, delicate stitchery capturing the flora and fauna of a dozen exotic worlds. Out of the corner of his eye, Homes saw Bryant stiffen. The veteran's disapproval crackled through the air.

The second holo recorded in shocking detail the humiliating punishment to which Brown had been submitted. He sat on an overturned bucket (where did Bryant get *that* archaism?) dressed in the ill-fitting, ludicrous costume stained various—but equally distasteful—shades of blue. A small white cap perched on his newly shaven head. He was inexpertly whittling away at the outer rind of the tubers with the curiously shaped instrument. One knuckle bled profusely from the shredding it had received.

"Peeling potatoes," a voice whispered hoarsely from the back. "My God, I thought they were extinct."

"Mid-twentieth century K. P." another breathed. "How could he?"

Homes cleared his throat. No use wasting time. His duty was clear. He tapped the stylized ship's bell three times with the electropen.

"This court has reached a judgment. Captain C. B. Bryant is found guilty of Infringement of Personal Dignity and is ordered to make appropriate restitution. The case is clear-cut. A simple question of crewel... and unusual punishment."

ROOT...AND BRANCH

"Poor man! And just to think, a couple of years ago he showed such promise."

"Isn't it a shame," the other woman agreed, her stage whisper carrying forcefully through the omni.

Patrick Bearns glanced up surreptitiously from the textreel he was scanning. Outside, a sad, drooping figure huddled against the neo-brick of a freshly boarded-over building. Patrick had seen the derelict around town, on occasion had even passed him in the streets without paying much attention. Today, however....

Patrick studied the man covertly. It would not do to be seen watching too closely. Legally there was nothing held against the man. After all, his genetic makeup wasn't his fault. But socially.... That was another question.

In the seat ahead of Patrick, the two old women continued their mock-whispered dialogue.

"I wish they could do something about people like that. It's so...so...."

"...so unrefined," the second said, completing her companion's unstated thought.

"Yes, dear. So *unrefined* to allow them to loiter

around like that. I would think that even *those* kind should be of *some* use to society...." The voice trailed off into an overt and wholly ungenerous stare.

Patrick blinked against the sun as the omni paused, waiting for the traffic impulse to re-activate the accelerator. The man outside seemed oblivious to the omni, to the few walkers passing silently in front of him. He stared blankly at a spot on the pavement, his unshaven cheeks pale and hollow, his jumpsuit too large, unpressed, stained dark blue around the neck and under the arms.

Patrick raised his eyes. The man was too painful a sight, right now at least. Abstractedly, Patrick studied the building behind the derelict, tracing the lines of a series of hastily hammered boards over a shattered plate-glass window. Wait a minute now...yes! He smiled at the perfect, accidental irony.

The building was one of the See-er hideouts Gov agents had found not over a day or two before. Patrick had noted the headlines on the scanner. Rumor that it that thousands of gen-records (curiously distorted, perversely inverted, but then that was usual with See-er records) had been seized and carted off. It must have been an exciting time for this corner for a few hours.

Somewhere ahead, a mechanical mind closed a relay. The omni purred into life, pulling away from the figure leaning against the hollow See-er chapel. With a darting movement, Patrick swiveled his head once for a final surveying glance. The man could be...oh, as old as thirty or as young as....

Patrick refused to finish the thought. He was nearly nineteen, just a few months beyond his legal coming of age. Possibly, within a year, he might be standing on a corner, hunching against a cold, impersonal pile of neo-bricks as an omni passed by. He shuddered.

But at least he had been saved a worse fate. He smiled wryly again at the essential irony of the figure leaning against a *See-er Chapel* (it was infuriating how they could establish their secret corners even in the busiest parts of town—and get away with it for months). The *See-ers* of all people! A couple of them had cornered Patrick once, maybe six or seven months before. He had heard of them, of course (who hadn't, considering how *odd* they were) but had never actually met one. Not until the two fellows sat down beside him on the omni that day and had cautiously begun a discussion of religion. Patrick should have jumped up immediately and denounced them, but he had been young and foolish— not quite so foolish as today, though—and had decided to listen. Most of it was interesting, even occasionally fascinating. And there wasn't actually anything wrong with *believing* in such oddities as angels and miraculous books and visions and See-ers. In fact, some of the ideas sounded...well, somehow *right*. But then they had stopped, sort of flushed, shuffled a bit with their well-worn shoes, and started talking about *Gen-scan*. Patrick couldn't tell for sure, but it almost sounded as if the two were *against* gens! They kept using old-fashioned words like 'family' and 'ancestor' until finally Patrick could stand it no longer. He did jump up, not to report the subverters, but to run away. And that time, too, he had thrust a quick glance backward, only to see a look of intense, inexplicable sadness shifting across the two fellows' faces.

Just remembering that incident made him nervous. And now, to pass by one of *their* places and see the derelict standing there....

"There but for the grace of gen go I," he muttered.

One of the old ladies turned her head, glaring at him from the impervious dignity of a long, thin nose.

"What, my dear? Were you speaking to us?"

"No, ma'am."

The woman turned back to her companion, the momentary interruption entirely forgotten.

"I've seen his four-gen profile," she stated, self-satisfied and not a little triumphant.

"No! But Tilda, that's illegal. Nobody sees the profiles except the subject. And the researcher, of course. They're held in the *strictest* confidence!"

"Well," Tilda said, smirking as if conscious of a small victory over her friend and eager to exploit it. "My cousin Sara works in Records, and she sneaked out a whole *packet* of files, mostly failures like him. Why, you'd be shocked at what his gen-scan is like— adulterers, murderers, a-govs, thieves."

The other woman paled, clutching theatrically at a polymer brooch, inscribed with the golden ladder of Records, clasped angularly across the bosom of her jumpsuit.

"It's true," Tilda said authoritatively. "Gov only

knows what else might be let loose on society if people like that were allowed to breed. Why, even some who have passed the gen-scan, for instance, like y—"

"Oh Tilda! You haven't...."

Patrick's attention slipped away from the impending crisis between the women as a red light on the panel in front of him winked a warning. His module was about to separate. He pulled in his legs (a needless gesture but deeply comforting) as a plexi-panel slid between himself and the seat in front of him, isolating him from the women. His module—half-a-dozen seats, mostly empty—split from the parent omni, turned sharply to the right, and slid up a steep ramp toward a shadowed opening.

The building approached rapidly. Patrick swallowed hard, his fingers thrumming nervously on the padded seat beside him.

His Dorm-brothers were right. He was a fool. To be suckered into such a dare! And only a few weeks after he had been so idiotic as to mention his brief meeting with the See-ers. And (trust his big mouth) he had *had* to mention his feelings that there might be some truth in their claims. Talk about unmerciful razz-ings! When would he ever learn? It would serve him right if the gen-search *did* turn up social deviates and mental weaklings. He was an adult (well, almost) and should have more self-control and far less gullibility. He shouldn't have lost his temper yesterday, not even when Marc had goaded him so unmercifully.

"Afraid, Bearn? Who knows what you'll find out

when your parents are identified? Idiots? Defects? Maybe even a See-er Prophet?"

Someone else picked up the taunt. "Hey, I'll bet he comes from old Bigamy Young's brood. And everyone knows what their gen-scans are like!"

"No!" Even now Patrick blushed at the memory of his voice breaking like an eight-year-old's. "My genes are as...better than yours could ever be. My parents were...my...they had to be.... Anyway, you can't know who *you* are either!" What a stupid, childish cut—so ineffectual that even as he had said it he had burned crimson watching the jeering faces of his Dorm-brothers. "None of you do! None of you do!" he had screamed, aware immediately that he had lost—both his temper and the battle. He had said the unsayable, emphasized the obvious—but that had not answered the charge of cowardice against him. He would show them, he would....

"I'm not afraid. I'm going in tomorrow! *Tomorrow*!"

The ring of laughing faces fell silent. Many people lived long, happy lives of bachelorhood before initiating the mandatory gen-searches at age forty. Patrick was about to gamble away precious years of his life.

"Hey, Pat," Marc began, "you don't have to. We were just...."

Patrick had shrugged his arm away as Marc reached out to touch him. "I'm going in tomorrow."

Well, it was tomorrow and the gen-search HQ towered over him, a monolith of the ubiquitous neo-bricks, featureless and intimidating. Soon he would know. His taunt echoed hollowly now—"You don't know, either. None of you do!" Not exactly accurate, at least not if the rumors about the See-ers were true. They were supposed to have huge caches of secret records, birth and death records going back thousands of years, although why they were so adamant about keeping the data in the face of the persecution of the past few Govs, Patrick could not tell. Searching out bloodlines seemed a little thing to die for.

Then he stiffened. That was precisely what *he* was doing. Oh, not the same way, not archaically, poring over disintegrating, dusty, filthy books to go farther and farther back. No, not like that. But essentially he was putting his life on the line, too. If his gen-scan didn't prove out, he would be as much an outcast as any fanatical See-er.

The module slowed, stopped outside the entryway. One panel slid back as Patrick stood up. His foot caught on a slip of paper and he knelt absently and picked it up before stepping out of the omni. He didn't hear the module hiss away as he meticulously unfolded the scrap. (One part of his mind correctly identified the delaying tactic and sent waves of guilt flooding through him: "Get in there and do it, you coward. Quit wasting time!") He smoothed the paper.

It was a tract, worn and rather poorly printed. Patrick had to squint to make out the wording. *Church of Jes....* See-ers! As if ashamed, he crumbled the paper again and tossed it to the pavement. And he was ashamed, although he could not quite place why. He almost turned back.

But the gen-scan meant more. He had to show those Dormies that he was a man. He climbed the dozen low steps, his mind ticking off each one funereally, dolefully, as if each intoned the death of youth. Or of... something not quite understood, not quite perceived but precious.

Inside, the building was curiously warm. He would have thought that the darkness and the solid façade of neo-brick would have insulated it better than that. Somewhere, machinery droned, whispered dully in still air. He felt depressed and foolish and afraid.

There were no lines. That was a break, at least. He followed a muted grey arrow down one corridor, turned left, continued through a hallway studded with closed, unmarked doors, and then turned right. A long counter closed off nearly an entire end of a wide reception room. Behind the counter, five clerks assiduously maintained the illusion of busy-ness. Patrick picked out the friendliest looking, a woman only a few years older than himself, with soft hair and eyes that glistened in the artificial light. Unconsciously he straightened.

"Name?" she asked in a voice entirely uninflected and cold.

"Patrick Bearn."

"Age?"

"Nin..., um, eighteen and ten."

"Status?"

"Single. Dorm 43B. Student."

The answers came naturally, easily. Until the gen-search was completed he had no other identity.

"Marriage-permission search?"

"No."

For the first time the clerk looked up at him.

"Fatherhood out of marriage?"

"N-n-no," he stuttered, angry at his lack of planned sophistication for the question he knew would come. "I just want a personal search. I want…I want to know *who* I am," he blurted out, aware of the inherent triteness of the line.

She didn't laugh, as he had feared she might. In fact, her face hardened into a look of concern, almost fear.

"You're sure. After all, you're quite young. Don't you want to wait for a few…?"

"No!" He was afraid to let her continue, feeling the irritating conviction reappear. She was right. This was *not* the way. But he had no choice now. "I want to know."

"Certainly," she intoned, suddenly cold and official. "Gov finds pleasure in helping his sons discover who they are. Please take a seat over there. The technician will be with you shortly."

He studied the line of identical plastic contour chairs before carefully choosing the third from the left. He sat in it, stiffly and uncomfortably, unable to shake off the weight of doom. He didn't want to do this. She didn't want him to do this. Those two See-ers (why did he think of them *now*?) certainly wouldn't want him to do this. But he had to. He couldn't back out now and be a man.

Curiously, he had never thought about his gen-line before. He had always supposed that no one ever did. Infants were reared in Dorms, with occasional outing for up to a year in Fosters. Patrick's memories included three Fosters, friendly and loving at times he had particularly needed closeness. But he had never questioned himself about his *biological* heritage, about his "parents," those two anonymous beings who had provided him with the genetic code soon to be evaluated and judged. Theoretically, at least, if his parents were allowed to bear children, then he should be...well, at least acceptable. But there were often exceptions. He remembered the derelict on the corner.

"Bearn."

The voice startled him. He jumped up, standing rigidly, just a breath this side of full military attention. Gov trained well.

"This way," a tech muttered, nodding ambiguously toward two doors. Patrick followed.

The test was anticlimactic. His ident had already been fed into the terminal. The tech placed a small tube in the hollow of Patrick's arm. A hiss of air, a small pricking—and the tech withdrew the tube, sticking an adhesive label on the gleaming surface.

"Blood sample," he noted absently, as if in answer to Patrick's questioning glance.

Then, "That's it." He slipped the tube into a delivery slot.

"That's all?" Patrick had always envisioned something more ...exotic, more sophisticated and complex.

"Just the blood. From that we get all the info we need for S&E. Search and Evaluation," he added when Patrick looked uncertain. "And, if necessary, a Scan."

Patrick swallowed. *Let there be a Scan. Oh, Gov, let there be a Scan.* Anything less meant oblivion, loneliness, ostracism. And he was only eighteen and ten.

He stood, rolled down the sleeve of his suit, and left. The girl did not look up as he walked in front of her on his way out.

The day had warmed. He decided to walk back to the corner to pick up the omni, rather than waiting for a module. Anyway, he needed to be alone. What he had just done was irrevocable. His whole life would change on the basis of the next few....

A figure moved up beside him. No, two. He looked up. He couldn't remember if they were the same two as before, but he thought so.

"What do you want?" he asked roughly, masking his sudden...what was it? Not fear exactly. He had no reason to *fear* them. After all, he was in control. All he had to do was yell, "See-ers!" and the gov-men would be there in seconds. So it wasn't fear. But he felt an inner turmoil. He didn't know how to define it and he wasn't sure he liked it. But then he wasn't sure he disliked it, either. Confusing.

"Did you?" the taller of the two began, gesturing with a sharp movement of his head toward the HQ.

"Yes. I had my search. What's it to you, anyway? Tomorrow, or the next day, I'll know who I am, what I am, and what I am to become. Leave me alone."

The taller one seemed sad. "But we could have told you that. Sooner, quicker, and more truthfully. If you would only listen to us for a few minutes...."

"Can't gotta run now." Patrick pointed to the omni pulling up, punctual as always. "Luck." He ran the last few steps, swung onto the omni platform, and slid his ident into the slot. He glanced at his watch, then at the schedule posted above the door. His watch was fifteen seconds slow. He punched the correct time, then found a seat in the proper module. When he looked out the window, the two young men were gone.

He was just beginning to forget them and relax when a voice filtered to him from across the aisle.

"...had his done last week. It was pretty good—a couple of medicians, an artist, by Gov even a gen-tech. But mine now! I've never seen one as good if I do say so myself. Third generation—engineers, a prize-winning physicist (working on gen-scan, they think). And the fourth gen is even more impressive."

Patrick turned his head and refused to listen. He couldn't take the man's quasi-illegal bragging right now, not when he didn't know what *his* search would discover.

The next days were painful. Three days of darkness, longer than he had anticipated, slower than eternity. The Dorm-brothers avoided him, as if they already knew that he would be leaving, an outcast, condemned by the life-stuff in his own cells. Marc couldn't meet Patrick's eyes, not even long enough to apologize again. And the word had spread. Even the girl's wing stayed unusually quiet when he passed along the row of half-open windows. Everyone knew. Everyone waited the decision. It would be—almost literally—continued death-in-life or a resurrection into society.

The message arrived during lunch. "Patrick Bearn. Gen-HQ. 14:00."

The same clerk was on duty. Patrick stepped hesitantly up to her, barely noticing that today she had changed her hair color. He cleared his throat.

"Yes?"

"Bearn." He thrust the scrap of message toward he. She flicked a glance at it, filed it in a small box, and gestured emptily with a stylus. "Take a seat."

He avoided the third chair from the left.

The room seemed to have grown smaller during the intervening days. And this time, it wasn't a tech who called his name. Patrick looked up to see a full-rank scanner gesturing to him. He stumbled out of the seat, his heart thrumming with sudden, irrational anticipation.

The woman said nothing as they walked along a short corridor toward an office brightly papered in yellow, with amorphous landscapes scattered across one wall.

"Please sit down, Mr. Bearn," she said, her voice modulated for maximum politeness.

His breath quickened. Good news! It had to be!

"Your gen-search was quite impressive," she said. He closed his eyes. The background susurration of machinery grew to a roar, filling his ears. He had passed. He had passed! All that worry for nothing. He had passed!

"Mr. Bearn?"

His eyes flew open and he straightened. "Uh, yes?"

"As I was saying, your maternal grandparent was the commander of the First Mars Colony, a brilliant scientist and...."

He bit at his lip. *Hurry,* he pleaded silently, *skip these irrelevancies.* He didn't care anymore about his parents or his grandparents, he suddenly realized—and he had *never* really cared about them. Leave them to the See-ers, with their useless prattle about *family* and *love* and *unity* and *eternal bonds.* Society simply could not function on such concepts. Society had to be governed and controlled, and genetic lines were important only in establishing the potential of each individual for service to society. Hadn't he known that since he was an infant, hadn't he heard Gov speaking to him night and day from posters and billboards, radios, textreels, whispers and barking orders supported by long black rifles. Let the See-ers have them, those dim ancestors relegated to a useless, unalterable past. They were of no use to him now. *Hurry and give me my four-gen reading, now!*

He interrupted the scanner. "What about me?"

She smiled. "Your natal pattern was, of course, approved and on file. And no abnormalities showed up in the blood sample. They do, sometimes, you know."

He nodded idiotically, automatically, incapable of controlling the rocking of his head.

"As I said, no abnormalities. You immediately qualified for procreation. Here are the results."

She slid a thin graph screen to him.

He thumbed through it, understanding nothing until he got to the last page. He glanced at it, then looked up at her.

She smiled even more sweetly.

"You realize, Mr. Bearn, that we are dealing here with probabilities, not absolute realities. And that we do not disclose *any* information on the first gen to avoid even the slightest possibility of parental tampering with the offspring's grid, should a parent somehow—illegally"—her voice became momentarily grim, threatening, then relaxed—"illegally gain access to natal records. Still, given these limitations, your evaluation was surprisingly positive.

"There is a 90% probability that among your grandchildren, you will have a scattering of IQ's in the high 180's, as well as a number of medicians, administrators, educators, and scientists, as the graph you have indicates."

He looked at the grid screen. There was his present, his future—*who he was!*—a series of points connected by jagged lines on a screen. That was him! The dare had paid off.

"I shouldn't say this," and here she leaned conspiratorially over the desk to gesture with one manicured nail toward a particular name on the fourth listing, near the bottom of the screen. "And this is in strictest confidence, but I shouldn't be surprised to see a Continental

President among your great-great grandchildren. What a blessing for your posterity. I did this gen myself, and *I* should know."

She leaned back, still smiling.

Patrick traces an invisible pattern across the grids of the last screen, his finger surprisingly controlled. The haunting vision of the man on the corner faded, of the two See-ers and their odd effect on him. Patrick Bearn would have children, and his children's children's children would call Society blessed, would contribute to the strength and stability of Gov and Society. He would never see them, of course (and he felt a faint twinge at the thought, then quickly squelched it), and he would certainly never know them—but to know *that* they would be and *what* they would be…well, that was to know everything.

The scanner was speaking again.

"You will be contacted at the appropriate time concerning your optimum mate. I might note that the meeting is still some years in the future. The young lady is already quite attractive, however, and I think you will be pleasantly surprised. Until then, if you have any questions, please contact me. My reel."

She handed her business-reel to him, at the same time retrieving the grid screen.

"Confidential," she assured him. "These never leave the premises. You may, of course, refer to your own gen-scan if you wish, although most people wisely prefer to remain silent." Patrick remembered the loud-mouthed man on the module and the two gossiping old women. He would never be like that, he promised himself. "Except the special information I gave you," the scanner continued. "That must remain secret between you and me—your new identity, as it were, ensuring your place in the future."

She smiled again.

Patrick stood and thanked her.

Outside, the sun was warm, bright, inviting. He felt almost light enough to fly. He nearly danced down the corridor to the main trafficway.

He did not notice the two young men who followed a few paced behind him.

"It isn't who you are that counts," he murmured complacently, falling into the automatic patterning of the most recent gen-search slogan, "It's who your descendants are."

This time his watch was accurate to the second as the omni slid up to the corner and waited patiently to engulf him.

He didn't bother looking back. And thus he missed the look on the two See-ers' faces—the look of infinite sadness suffused with eternal, struggling hope.

THE GRAND EXPERIMENT

The old man was immensely powerful, immensely wealthy, and immensely protective of his privacy. No one entered the dome deep in the Alaskan wilderness without his permission, no one walked in the greenhouses where orchids bled vibrant purple against Arctic snows, no one touched priceless treasures in his private museum. And no one, *no one* on the outside knew of the five-year-old boy, motherless, reproduced from a single cell drawn from the old man's body. Or at least, no one was supposed to.

Security was absolute, which only intensified the mystery. The barrage of attendants, nurses, doctors did not see the boy solemnly stuff an assortment of *his* treasures into a plas-fab pillow case: a bright butterfly frozen in layers of acrylic; a miniature toiletry set with carved golden unicorns; a shapeless lump of alloy that glittered like the auroras when held to the light just so. No one saw him solemnly set out to "'splore" the world of white just beyond the tropical gardens.

And thus the mystery. A few tiny footprints impressed in fresh snow as the trail led away from the protection of an unattended airlock. The search continued for hours…days; but fruitlessly. One of the searchers found what he thought were skicycle tracks intersecting the boy's and followed the single set of indentations until the wind obliterated them.

When the search was called off, only one solid, unmistakable remnant of the boy's presence had been found. A searcher discovered it all but buried in a drift just outside the airlock, where it must have fallen from the child's hoard—all that remained of the grand experiment: the gold brush of the Alaskan clone-tyke.

MATING QUEST

"Curse the witch. Curse her forever!"

Blanchard's voice, hoarse with bitter black bile, nonetheless cut like a laser beam through the silence of the rock-choked gorge. He could identify the treble whine of hysteria in the sound, a thin, high keening for all that had passed, a dirge for the unknown that was to be. One part of his mind—long isolated, almost decayed—relayed a crisp warning: "Insanity!" Blanchard accepted the assessment without argument—after all, who could argue with fact—and bowed to the inevitable before blanking it out, retreating into the psychosis of his loneliness.

"Curse her forever!"

He was alone…had been alone now for…how long was it? He glanced sullenly at the line of quavering hatch marks marching irresolutely across a stained fragment of paper. Two…no, three days ago the mechano-pen had finally quit, its dying splotches spreading irregularly through the coarse filament. The last three lines were gouged roughly into the paper with a sharpened twig, fire-hardened and ashen-grey. He counted the marks slowly, carefully, as if his remaining threads of sanity were somehow irrevocably bound up with those vestiges of a human past. Each line brought him back further in time, closer to the others—to when there had been others. Weeks. Months. He blinked convulsively to clear his eyes. Dead. All dead,

"And I only am escaped alone to tell thee." He laughed again; the note of hysteria had climbed higher, had become a piercing wail shattering off the corroded granite cliffs on each side. He noted the fact almost clinically.

He was shaken by the awful appropriateness of the ancient quotation.

He stumbled on, each breath a nightmare of fiery agony, each step almost impossible until achieved. He did not look behind him to the uneven floor of the valley. In the distance, over his left shoulder, three arabesques of murky smoke curled baroquely from tall, thin towers, then spread miasmally across the landscape like webbing extruded from monstrous spinnerets. The faintest fringes of the deadly carpet lapped angrily at his boots, but he did not notice; he had not consciously noticed the vapors for days now. Behind him, nothing grew in the noxious fumes. Here and there standing revenants of organic growth—now cold, dead, unchanging—bore witness to the deadly poisons unwittingly released by her idiotic—criminally idiotic—tampering with the normal ecological balances of the colony-planet. One microscopic enzyme had escaped from the lab...somehow...and— voila!— Paradise transmuted into hell.

Yes, he nodded manically, paradise into hell—and humanity into something no longer quite human.

A

The last planet, the last hope, loomed emerald and cerulean, its sphere studded and overshadowed by browns and misted in a vaporous veil. It would do...it must! NumFeir, the last of the ancient Sy'ayes wrapped themselves more tightly in their gossamer, shivering in anticipation. The two amorphous nuclei in their shared being throbbed with eagerness...and desperation. This would be the final chance. If it failed...oblivion for the lone surviving doubling of the Sy'ayes.

The craft, an elongated needle-like vessel of a substance as iridescent as oil upon water, slid through the upper atmosphere, glowing slightly for a moment, then cooling, settling without incident onto a broken ridge of rock overlooking a narrow valley. The sensors had determined that this would be the optimum site for a landing; here, for some curious reason, the essential oxides, sulfides, hydrocarbons were literally so concentrated as to be visible to the unaided receptors of the Sy'aye. NumFeir sniffed hopefully at a tiny flask, savoring the almost forgotten odors of the home planet duplicated almost miraculously here, on this distant world. For some forms of life, they realized, this planet promised only death.

But for the Sy'aye, that death could mean life. Could.

2

Blanchard stumbled onward, impelled by precious fears and nightmare hopes he could no longer segregate or name. Higher! Higher! Out of the valley of death (but there was no escaping that, he reminded himself bitterly—at least his isolated, scientific, sane part did, glancing at the mists bathing his boots), out of the valley of death and up to the blinding flash of white that had flared momentarily, promising death and final destruction, before paling to the uniform grey of the clouds.

"Curse the witch!" he screamed, trilling consonants with malicious glee. "She died...why can't I!"

A fragment of chloride-green shale beneath his feet separated from the ridge, from its precarious niche between the granite walls, twisted twice, and shuddered down the slopes. Blanchard lurched forward, scrabbling for a hand hold. He barely noticed as sharp edges of shale sliced across the palms; his blood dotted torn flesh, coagulating almost immediately. Lacerations slashed his exposed flesh already—a few more would pass unnoticed. He flung his right arm wide, struggling to grasp the rough edges of a granite outcropping, but the slope continued to give way. He slipped, then tumbled inertly on the sliding shale, back down the slope so laboriously traversed, back to the floor of the valley.

He pulled himself to his knees, the fury of madness subsiding and dying before a cold, calculating control. He brushed ineffectually at the tattered shreds of his trousers, and began climbing again.

B

What think you, Num? Feir's feminine impulses swept softly through shared neural circuits as she communicated with her male doubling. Will it succeed?

I cannot say yet, Num replied instantaneously, but we must try, or die!

Feir pulsed her assent. They moved somberly toward the airlock, the shimmering silver of their gossamer thickening, coarsening, and coalescing around themself to protect them from the unbreathable oxygen atmosphere high on the ridge crest, an atmosphere as poisonous to the Sy'aye doubling as the mutagens in the valley had proven to the native vegetation.

Silently, as if a morning mist upon the land, the Sy'aye floated free of the ship to begin their descent. Neither spoke; they had passed beyond language in the depths of their emotional response to the planet they had—at last, and beyond all reasonable hope—found. But threading between them, implicit in the membranous tissues of their shared gossamer were bitter memories of a homeland destroyed by an errant solar flame lashing out from a once-friendly sun....

Once there had been many Sy'ayes. The homeland was mantled in fogs and vapors, spawning Sy'aye doublings in countless thousands. Emerging from the bodypouches of the male singlings, the doublings rose like fragile opalescent bubbles in the mists of spring, two microscopic nuclei sharing a single gossamer. Nourished by the soup of chemicals in the mists, the doublings grew, intimately connected, male and female, ever joined—yet ever separated by the gossamer. And with the years they matured, became as one in mind and spirit, sharing all...except the final union the mating quest would bring.

At the end of their seventeenth season, Sy'aye doublings migrated, floating sinuously southward from the pole toward the muggy, torrid central highlands. As the doublings tumbled on the autumn airswells, their nuclei darkened, solidified, and struggled against the filaments separating them, until the colder currents from the north collided with super-heated air rising from the sulfurous fires of a ring of volcanoes banding the planet.

Then, entrapped in a private hurricane, buffeted and pitched crazily through an atmosphere made insane, each doubling pivoted and swirled, growing sluggish and inert as the volcanic fumes penetrated the gossamer and chemical reactions dispassionately severed intimate bondings that had remained inviolable since birth.

And then—oh glory! ecstasy of pain beyond all words! agony of joy inexpressible!

The gossamer becomes granular, elongates, pulls apart, separates in the ancient rite, rending neutrons, dividing substance, creating ...singlings veiled in fine, tenuous tendrils which harden into fingers, sensitive and impressively manipulative. The singlings draw near, touch, and join, merge in the mating quest...

then separate once more—finally and for all time—to generate the race anew.

It was glorious, magnificent...and now utterly destroyed.

Few doublings had survived. The flare had given them little warning—at first light that day, the sky had been tinged with a fiery fury beyond the recollections of the eldest singlings. The air, normally warm and humid, was parching, witheringly hot. And the sun, when it finally rose beyond the mists, was distorted and twisted, hot beyond all imagining. The nurturing mists dissipated with the first touch of the heat, baring the homeland's private parts, hidden before in the perpetual vapors. Moist black soil died in a breath, cracking into irregular plates before dissolving into dust. Deep patches of velvet moss crisped in the heat. Most of the singlings were stuporous from shock and despair; only a handful appreciated the full meaning of the phenomenon glaring balefully down on them. They herded what doublings they could into a drone ship, newly returned from an exploratory mission to the homeland's nearest neighboring planet, and chittered to the pulsating bubbles in tones co-mingled of fear and resignation: Flee, save the race! It matters not that we die. We are old. You are young and must survive. Flee!

The doublings did. Into the depths of space they fled, leaving behind all that they knew of life. The scanners focused on the homeland at the final moment, as the great arm of flame reached out to embrace an insignificant, spinning clot of matter—to embrace and destroy it. Then the scanners died and the doublings faced the unknown, leaving behind a charred world, a fleck of ash in the velvet void. Before them stretched infinities.

And there the doublings died, deprived of hope, deprived of those elements which sustained and strengthened them for the separation. They died, until only four remained, then three, finally one—NumFeir of the ancient Sy'ayes.

3

"Curse her! Curse her! Curse her'" The contrapuntal litany established its own living rhythm as he scrabbled painfully up the slope.

At the beginning, no one had noticed her one moment of devastating negligence; the enzyme had escaped, inadvertently allowed to infiltrate the cooling system at the labs, then flushed unknowingly with inert wastes into the streamlet ambling near the base of the plasteel structure. In the beginning, no one had noticed; toward the end, no one could ignore its consequences. No one was immune, either. The lucky ones had died quickly, painlessly, as the chemical reactions began—unpredictably and unalterably, damaging beyond anything analogous on industrial Earth. The less fortunate had survived...changed. Marya had literally become a walking computer as the altered atmosphere invaded her brain, re-arranging neural circuits and patterns; but her flesh had sagged, eaten away by hideous lesions and cancers. Jono could establish telepathic links with any one of the colony's dwindling inhabitants; but his eyes had dissolved overnight. For each mental advance, a physical debilitation...each surpassing the last in horror.

Blanchard shook his head viciously, trying to jar loose the memories he stored. "Curse her! Curse her! Curse her!" drummed continually as his heart beat more violently. The ridge crest was nearing. Soon now.

His mind slipped again unnoticed into unwanted remembrance.

Blanchard had seemed immune to the combined mutagens as the chemical reactions became self-perpetuating, replicating wildly in the atmosphere. Had seemed, but was not. All that he had exchanged for his continued good health was—increasingly, now almost continuously—his sanity. And she, SHE! She had twisted overnight, grown ugly, an obscene parody of the beauty he had married. Her mind went, too, except for those selected synapses which allowed her to peer Cassandra-like into the future. Blanchard and the others had laughed, mocked, disbelieved—but she had been right each time. One by one, her fatal words became insane realities, bringing first disfigurement and disability...then death. Each time but one. He would father no children now. He would not live to see his flesh renewed, as she had croaked in her final, failing breath. He was alone. He could not...would not even if he could. So he defied her prophecy, fleeing the remnants of the settlement where the ghosts hung stiffly in the poisonous sky. He defied her gift, running wildly from her and from himself. You shall be the father of the renewal. You shall see your children, though you know them not.

"No! No!" He strained up the sheer precipice of the shale slagheap that had been a mountain. He screamed incessantly, not hearing himself. The steely clouds rang now with curses, now with imprecations, now with useless pleas and tear-filled prayers. He dared the slope to do its worst; he flaunted his desire for death, half-believing now that she had been right. Horrifyingly right. He could not die.

Again the bedding rocks gave way, throwing him off balance. He fell backwards, striking his head against an outcrop more stable, less decomposed than the rest. Semi-conscious, he slid down to the valley floor, losing all of the ground he had gained at the cost of immense struggle. Through misty eyes, he watched the crest ride higher and higher away from him. Up there...there was something up there! A flash, an intimation of intense heat. It was too early for the supply ship—months and years too early, since the colony had been self-sufficient for over a year before the last ship had arrived. But there was something. Perhaps there, on all of the colony-world, he would find that which would accept his offer of death.

For a few moments he lay still, crumpled at the base of the slope, a formless mass of matter huddled against the jagged womb of a planet. He drifted through more levels of consciousness than he could have ever imagined, looking up once to see her coming toward him, floating toward him, trailing wisps of that lavender filminess he had once given her on another world, in another time.

Then he fell back again, mercifully unconscious.

C

NumFeir floated toward a dead valley on the last of many planets. There would be no more planets, they reminded themselves bitterly. Meager supplies would not suffice for another branching through space, nor would the life-force inherent in the gossamer. Already oxygenated molecules were seeping through the protective filaments; NumFeir could sense subtle, almost subliminal alterations in their physical makeup. Yes, this place would be the last home of the Sy'ayes. Here they would live or die, but they would never again be the same, never again take to the emptiness beyond in search of a new homeland. This would be the end, one way or another.

The ship's memories had chattered of hope, however. The pockets of vapor adorning the planet's surface had scanned properly—just the right combination of chemicals, moisture, and heat, all that was required for the division of one into two which preceded the mating quest. As yet, the pockets were relatively small and localized, but the computer assured them that the vapors were spreading, fingering across the face of the planet. And now they were moving deep into the largest of the pockets, testing conditions, defining the atmospheric changes occurring around them.

If it is sufficient, Feir pulsed, I shall soon see you as singling, my one.

And if not, Num responded, let us die co-joined, forever ignorant of the joys of singling.

An eddy fluttered through the gossamer, stirring cells and triggering responses long feared forgotten. NumFeir flushed in anticipation. Did you feel that, Feir intoned carefully, struggling to keep unwarranted hope from the tones.

I did. It was as a breath of the Homeland, it was like the beginning winds of….

Just so, Feir interrupted. Just so. And we may hope.

Without hesitation, they roiled down the uneven surface toward the valley floor.

4

Blanchard moaned softly as consciousness returned fully. He blinked once, twice. Distortions wavered in front of his eyes. He was lying at an angle to the incline of the slope and everything—rocks, clouds, ridges, crest—canted dizzyingly to the right. A brief flash of crystal sanity pierced his mind, urging him to stop, to think, to reconsider and return. Perhaps in the abandoned lab at the settlement…indeed, only in the abandoned lab at the settlement might there be hope that he could….

"Curse her!" The scream interrupted, thrusting him again into the darkness of her prophecies. He whirled wildly, trying to orient himself. At first he saw only blurriness as his mind wheeled in and out of control. He was back again at the beginning, one of half a thousand, buoyant with hope and expectations for this paradise world...now there were only fifty, scarred and ravaged, huddling in a close circle in the evening glow—violently scarlet glow—of the colony's sun, and he among them, listening against his will to the garbled words of the thing that had once been his wife. She crouched low on the ground, enshrouded in shadows, as if she were a living protrusion of the soil itself. And she muttered endlessly, repetitiously her warnings, defined her visions from dusk to dusk, never ceasing. He had not wanted to listen to her; no one had. But there was no way to defy the weirding quality of that hideous voice, and so he, like the other survivors, had squatted near her, hating himself as he did so yet listening to her words. It was like eavesdropping on a nightmare. Only this nightmare was his, everyone's, as well as hers. And now he was standing alone above the matted lump of dirty rags obscuring her twisted body. He was watching dispassionately as the mass heaved and trembled, even now throwing out a vagrant word, unintelligible in content yet easily readable in emotion. She was still caught inextricably in the web of her mutation; he had hoped, irrationally he supposed, that at the end her mind would clear as others' minds had, that he could re-affirm once again his love for the woman imprisoned in the altered flesh. And then the trembling had eased and a single, terrible cry had echoed from the stillness at his feet.

He had turned and walked away.

"And I only am escaped alone to tell thee."

Blanchard shook his head violently, clearing it of vestigial memories. All of that was in the past. His calendar of rude scratches on the piece of paper proved that he was alone and had been alone for...he dug into one pocket for the scrap, then paled and felt frantically over his ragged clothing when he could not find the paper. He couldn't have lost it! It was his only link with what had been! And without it he was truly alone, absolutely isolated in both space and time from himself as he had been.

He forced himself to calm down, to stare at a single slick glint of mica for interminable seconds until his heart slowed down. It must have fallen out, he assured himself, when I fell down the slope. Therefore it must be up there somewhere. He shaded his eyes with one hand and began tracing the path back up the ….

And he saw it.

As large as himself, whirling and shimmering with all of the life that he had believed forever drained from this world, it descended the slope, effortlessly, hardly even touching the shifting sand. Deep within the veiling luminescence, two points of purple pulsed. He shook his head, moaning.

It was a dream, a wild hallucination, anything but what it seemed.

And something deep within himself snapped, finally and irrevocably.

Blanchard raised his eyes again to the thing and saw her standing there, above him, mocking his attempts to escape, to elude the fate which her chemically enhanced prescience had determined. The amorphous shape became a human form, draped in diaphanous light...no, not a form, merely a face, two penetrating eyes, glowing and mocking....

He screamed and whirled, trying to run. The fragment of his mind that still struggled into partial sanity remonstrated disjointedly with the rest. *No, don't run. She is dead. You saw her die; you stood over her body, weeping and rejoicing, heart-broken and exultant. The body was a monstrosity, too alien to be touched or buried, true, but it is dead. Wait! Think!*

Too late. Blanchard exploded into a run, his feet slipping dangerously on the chloride-green shale. He twisted, ripped ligaments in his ankle, and fell. The rock cut deeply into his temple, releasing the pent-up, racing blood.

D   5

NumFeir floated downward, thrusting their imprisoned beings into the welcome, turgid vapor. As they descended, they felt more and more strongly the incipient pull of the gossamer as it attenuated. Yes, they flashed joyfully to each other, the computer had been correct. Conditions were correct...rather, they were ideal, improving geometrically as the Sy'aye moved closer to the valley floor. Soon, soon they would separate, become singlings.

The vapors thickened gradually.

Then NumFeir halted as a shape lying inert upon the

rocks shifted once and groaned.

What is it? Feir asked cautiously.

Num pulsed back immediately: *Indigenous life.*

The doubling hovered above the figure, examining it with extended wisps of gossamer.

Alive, Num flickered as a tendril touched lightly against the form, but injured. Dying. There may be danger. Should we go further?

We must, Feir answered, if we are to exist... here, or anywhere.

True.

The Sy'aye settled like a tactile dream upon the form, entered it, and probed....

E   6

There was pain as Blanchard surfaced to conscious levels from the darkness of his internal nightmares. It was an intense pain, accompanied by a weakness unlike anything he had ever experienced. He crushed his eyelids together, closing out the metallic light of the sun and focusing on his inward monitors. Head injured, perhaps seriously. He could feel the blood pulsing out onto the soil of the colony world—and wondered disinterestedly at that. His blood had been clotting almost immediately since...well, for a long time. It shouldn't be pooling around the rocks like this. And then he wondered at his wonder; it should be fear but it was not. He shifted slightly, trying to ease a sharp tension in his back. The movement pinched. Breath hissed once as he stifled a cry.

Suddenly he knew that he was not alone. Still he refused to open his eyes. The...thing he had seen. His saner portion predominated now, allowing his insane half to mask tortured nerves and mute the pain. He could think. The thing had been alien, after all, nothing ever spawned on a world of men.

At least not on any world he had once known, he reminded himself, aware even as he thought that the air he breathed was thin and acrid, that the soil beneath his hand was sterile. A mutation, perhaps, as unnatural as Marya had become, as Jona, as...as she had been at the end. And as he was.

With an effort of will, he opened his eyes.

The shadow was above him, hovering less than a hand-breadth from his chest. Pseudopodia of mist extruded from the main mass, filtering toward him and touching him tentatively, tenuously, before they retracted.

He held his breath, aware still of the blood flowing from his head wound. A weakness spread out from his brain. He tried to move one leg. Nothing. No movement, no feeling. His hands were helplessly immobile. Only the brain continued to function.

Perhaps, he thought half-triumphantly, yet still cowed by the authority of his dead wife's terrible vision, perhaps I can cheat her after all. And I will rest. Humanity will rest forever on this dead planet. We could not live in harmony with this world; perhaps by dying I can rectify the balance.

He closed his eyes again, waiting desperately for the

weakness to become total, for the blood to rush faster from his body and stain the ground crimson with its energy. He waited for the release she had denied him in her prophecies, but which was not imminent, inevitable, desired.

Then a choking gasp as they/it invaded. One. More than one. He could not distinguish clearly. But he could define their alien interest in himself. They/It spread through him, investigating muscles, tissues, cells. One touched his brain. He cried as he felt the explosion of vitality and life within his cells. He screamed, then fell back limp and lifeless on the rocks.

7F

The Sy'aye settled upon the form, entered it, and probed it, assimilating electrical charges defined as memories.

Pain! NumFeir shuddered as they shared the neural messages racing from the body toward the brain. Then suddenly the pain was not the alien creature's but their own. A twisting, wrenching pain shaded imperceptibly through greater agony to become even greater joy. The thing they had entered was dead, inert, but neither Num nor Feir noticed. Num was alone, one for the first time in his existence as he felt his nucleus ripping away the gossamer bands which had bound him inextricably to Feir. That for which they had been searching, hoping without true hope, was happening, and neither of the doubling had even noticed its onset; their interest in the alien had been so all-consuming that they had ceased to monitor themself. Yet even as their filaments had invaded the alien, the process had begun, altered and stimulated by chemical processes within the alien itself.

Num stretched and flexed gossamer tendrils as they joined and solidified into appendages, foreign-formed but somehow appropriate to this new world. He withdrew entirely from the alien's body, taking with him elements and substance around which the gossamer solidified according to genetic codings within each alien cell. Num saw his limbs differentiating...upper and lower extremities, in a bipedal arrangement wholly unlike the singling form assumed on the home planet, but admirably suited to this roughly textured place. The borrowed memories provided names: arms and legs, fingers and toes. Here there would be no strong air-currents to carry the doublings toward merging grounds; the legs of the singlings would have to provide that service. Num manipulated one of the lower limbs, half-stumbling, but keeping a precarious balance.

As he looked about him through eyes new-formed, he saw Feir. She was exquisite in her fragile beauty, clothed in the flesh of a female of the alien kind, attractive in a curiously appealing way. Her gossamer had not yet completely solidified. She shimmered like the opalescent mists of autumn on the home world.

∞

Num reached out to her, touched her in the passionate ritual of the mating quest.

"At last," Feir breathed, blushing at the tenderness in her virgin voice as it distilled through silences. "At last, a homeland."

Neither glanced down at the remains of the body they had entered, whose memories were now divided among their own, whose component atoms now supported new life. They did not stop to analyze the joy they felt in a world the alien had so despised and feared.

And hand in hand, the children of man walked toward the life-giving richness concentrated near the valley floor. This world had been empty. Soon it would burgeon with life. Life-from-death.

The World was all before them, where to choose
Their rest, and Providence their guide....

PACKAGE FROM HOME

Brett Hunt ran one finger along the thumblock of the bill of lading. In front of him, taking up most of the available warehouse space, the bio-pack from Colony Headquarters loomed in the dimness. Inside that plasteel container was the colony's salvation—or death warrant.

Months ago, Hunt had sent an urgent request to Col. HQ. Even with the latest developments in parthenogenesis restricting the need for males and expediting fertilization of ova more rapidly than would be possible naturally, the original livestock that the colony had been able to import desperately needed replenishing. Horses and sheep thrived on the coarse russet grass filling the hollows, but their numbers were insufficient for the colony's increasing needs. Even more seriously, the cattle and poultry refused any native foods at all; they were dwindling, dying almost daily.

So Hunt had forwarded computerized tapes to Col. HQ, pleading not only for additional horse and sheep embryos, but also for something—anything!—to replace the cattle and poultry. Since then, the entire settlement had waited nervously. If Col. HQ. agreed that the need was indeed urgent, there might still be a chance to save the colony. If not….

The bill of lading sat on the makeshift desk, unopened, intimidating, as Hunt took a deep breath. Then he reached over, slid one thumb along the nearly invisible seal, and withdrew his hand as the message unfolded. For a moment, he didn't trust his eyes to read the words.

Half a minute later, the nervous silence that hovered over the colony was ripped by a wild yell of exultation. From all corners, colonists half-ran toward the warehouse, where Hunt met them, dancing excitedly from foot to foot.

"We got it all!" he gloated. "Fertilized ova of horses, sheep embryos, and to replace the cattle and poultry, they sent deer—venison! —and fertilized pigeon eggs. We got it all!"

"You mean…," a voice began from somewhere in the growing cluster.

"Yep." Hunt replied triumphantly. "We got it all! Mare zygotes and doe zygotes and little lambs and dove eggs!"

CHAOS AND ANCIENT NIGHT

Kipp had been walking rapidly, rather carelessly, across the sandy flats between two lines of ridges. On any other world the slight humps would hardly classify as decent hills; on Daphnis, they seemed dizzyingly high, soaring meters into the still air. He had paid little attention to his steps, since there were no dangerous life-forms on the planet—indeed, most reports denied the existence of anything but the smallest pseudo-mammals, tiny herbivores that scrounged a feeble living by feeding on the narrow swaths of plant life along the borders of the rivers that cut periodically through the otherwise omni-present desert. Other than that, according to official reports, the planet was devoid of life, merely a ball of tawny earth laced with silver rivulets.

He had been away from camp for most of the day, Now, with the approach of evening, he was hurrying back. It was not wise to wander about on Daphnis after dark, the long-timers had warned. Not because of any predators, obviously, but because of the sinks—blisters that had formed beneath the thin surface of the planet. Occasionally the sinks were easily spotted, either because the skin of packed soil had fractured and fallen in on itself, leaving shallow crater-like depressions in the plains, or because the white-tones caps bulged slightly, creating gently sloping domes. More commonly, however, the only indication of a sink was the sepulchral whiteness of a patch of sun-hardened earth. Sometimes the cap would hold a man's weight; other times, the rock would splinter and shatter, throwing whatever was on top of it into the blister. Rarely did such falls kill. The broken bones and debilitating injuries that easily and frequently resulted, however, did. The planet was large and the only treasure it offered—the Moonblood gems—were scattered. If a single prospector were to meet with an accident, no one and nothing would be near to give aid.

So Kipp was hurrying back to his base camp before nightfall. Starlight was bright on Daphnis, but also misleading. Its silvery gleam disguised the white domes, and Kipp was not about to take chances.

He followed his earlier trail in the undisturbed sand, stopping occasionally to sip as he crossed the shallow branches of the main stream. When he came to one of his markers, he turned right and headed directly toward the nearest ridges. He squinted tightly against the glare. The light of the setting sun reflected blindingly off the mineral-strewn swellings of the ridges. He stumbled on, ducking his head, concentrating on the texture of the sand crunching beneath his boots. It was dusky brown, sturdy, stable. He was safe…so far.

A few moments later, he had left the plains and was climbing the nearest ridge. His feet no longer pounded on weathered sand. Instead they stumbled over rocks and boulders, picking out an invisible trail through a patch of shattered crystals. He leaned over the pick up one of the shards.

He hefted it, turned it over a few times. If only.... The shard was flawless, a smoothly lacteal white throughout, with just enough translucence to outline vaguely the forms of his fingers as he balanced it. He could trace silver threads through it, but there was no redness. White crystals were common and provided a fair market as a lubricant, no better and no worse than native products on a dozen other planets. They provided enough revenue to justify the expense of the space port and the single town, but no more.

But, he thought, if this gem were only tinged with that impossible scarlet. Once in a million times, the crystal was not white, was not milkily translucent, but rather glowed with an independent fire that highlighted the silvery strands within. Then the crystals became unendurably beautiful. Kipp had seen only one fine specimen, on display at the space port. He had seen it at first out of the corner of his eye, then had felt his head turn toward it, almost of its own volition. He had stood motionless, staring at the gem for...well, for some moments, at least. He had started when a voice pierced the silence.

"A real beauty, isn't it?"

"What is it," Kipp had asked, not even trying to keep

the awe from his voice.

"New here, aren't you?"

"Yes. This morning."

"That is a Moonblood gem of Daphnis."

The name had been fitting. Imprisoned within the single crystal were the heated fires of pulsing blood and the chaste purity of a virgin goddess, the flow of passion and the brilliance of ice.

"That stone alone could buy practically anything on Daphnis, including the space port itself," the old man continued. "Prospectors find, oh, maybe a hundred a year, out there in the back country, and none—I've heard—anywhere as fine as this one. A hundred in a year. Not much to supply a galaxy, is it."

Kipp had not answered but his love affair with the gem had begun. By evening he had decided to become a prospector. That had been two months and three small, deeply flawed gems ago.

He dropped the white crystal. He had already covered this flank of the ridge, without success. He turned his head toward the crest. Just beyond, in a little hollow, lay his base camp. In a few moments he would be home.

As soon as he cleared the crest, however, he could see that the camp was not as he had left it. His few possessions lay strewn about, his equipment in disorder around the cinders of last night's fire—a luxury he allowed himself only when camping near more plentiful sources of fuel. Beyond, disappearing into the darkness, the river looped sinuously to the north.

Under any other circumstances he would have been enraptured by its beauty. Now, however, he saw only one thing. Someone had raided his camp.

He rushed down the slope, skidding in the coarse detritus. He pulled up sharply at the edge of his camp, so sharply that he nearly hurled himself headlong into the cold ashes.

Panting, he searched, straining his eyes in the scant light. The gems were safe, he knew that, nor could he stop fingering the soft leather pouch tied securely about his throat, where the three flawed Moonbloods hung. They had been with him.

But other items were missing, many essential. Packs of food, salt pellets, several lanterns and force-knives—enough to make him furious, red-faced with anger. He had no idea that anyone was even in this sector, let alone so close as to sneak into camp after he left and raid it at leisure. Swiftly, he gathered the remnants of his kit, taking silent inventory, already figuring out how to do without this item or that. But the food packets and the salt…those he had to have. He had been warned about the dangers of the deserts, of the strenuous labors of prospecting. He would have to retrieve the salt pellets or head back to the port, losing valuable time.

He reached into the kit and pulled out his one remaining flash. He pressed the switch but no light penetrated the darkness. Cursing, he flung the useless hunk of metal on to the sand. No wonder the thief had left it. It was dead, and the recharger was missing. Any tracking would have to wait until morning.

Fighting his fury, Kipp forced himself to relax. He leaned against a sandy hillock and willed himself to sleep. He had always had the ability to sleep when and where…and for as long as he wished. The ability did not fail him.

At first light, Kipp awoke, leaped to his feet, instantly awake, neither hungry nor thirsty. First he would track down the thief, then….

He left the resolve unspoken. There would be time for that later. Now, he must find the man.

The still night had left the few scattered tracks undisturbed. Kipp was a fair tracker, having hunted for sport during layovers on a number of worlds. Now, however, there would be no sport. He was serious— deadly serious. No one would steal from him and get away with it.

Throughout the long day he kept to the trail, making good speed. The tracks continued, growing neither clearer nor more obscure. His quarry was making good time also. He was not stopping to use his new equipment. All day Kipp continued, oblivious to the landscape, to the escarpment of true mountains looming in the heat-hazed distance.

By nightfall, he congratulated himself on making some headway. The trail seemed a bit fresher, but that faint hope was enough to whet Kipp's hunger for the morning. Again he set his internal clock, relaxing into a deep sleep almost as soon as his head struck the coarse material of his kit. And again, he woke suddenly at the first hints of dawn.

By full light, he was well on his way, some kilometers from his resting place.

The terrain had changed subtly. There was less sand, more actual sod, barren for the most part of plant life, slightly moist, probably from the underground seepage of a river that surfaced nearby. The ground grew spongy, and the thief's tracks showed more plainly and clearly. Kipp increased his pace, often half-running over long stretches when the trail was sharp and well defined. With any luck….

His luck held. With still an hour or so of light left, Kipp approached a low ridge, not too different from the one where he had made his base camp. The trail was fresher than he had yet seen it; he knew instinctively that his quarry was near and—more importantly—not bothering to hide his tracks. They pointed straight to the crest.

Kipp climbed the shallow slope, careful not to loosen any telltale slides of gravel and stone. His fingers dug securely into the rock soil as he pulled himself up to the crest and slowly nudged his head over a line of nearly pulverized crystals.

There he was. A figure hunched over a small fire—a luxury indeed, since there was no visible plant life in this area. The man must have carried tinder and fuel with him. Kipp kept his eyes riveted on the dark form as he slid first one foot then the other down the crystal-studded slope. Noiselessly he approached, holding his force-knife at the ready.

He nearly stumbled when, not a dozen meters from the figure, a querulous voice croaked through the stillness.

"Took you long enough, boy."

Kipp started, then caught control of his nerves. Still unspeaking, he continued his approach. The figure moved, cocking his head over one shoulder to stare at Kipp.

"Heard you coming for the past half-hour. Made more noise than a gully-washer. Have a seat."

The old man gestured to a low clump of rocks nearby.

"I want my provisions. You stole them from me." Kipp tried to keep the quaver out of his voice. Somehow he had not quite expected this kind of reception. The old man's apparent unconcern left Kipp unnerved... and nervous.

"Stole? High-sounding words, eh? Found? Now I like that better. *Found.* Sitting out there on the desert, nobody around to lay claim to nothing. So I did. Found, yes; stole, no."

"They're mine," Kipp repeated, teeth clenched. If need be he would force this old man to give back his rightful property. "Food, salt, flashes, force-knives...."

He got no further.

The old man spun on his heels to face Kipp squarely.

"Listen, boy. Nobody orders me around. I find what I find. Nobody accuses me of stealing. Nobody."

Kipp pressed his warning home.

"I want my goods. I paid good money for them...."

Again the crackling voice interrupted.

"Paid!" the exclamation tapered off into a ringing laugh, high-pitched and forced. "Paid!"

With that the old man flicked his wrist, sending a brilliantly crimson stone spiraling through the air to land at Kipp's feet.

A Moonblood gem. A big one, perhaps even larger than the one at the port. Priceless beyond price anywhere but in the middle of this god-forsaken wilderness.

Kipp bent as if to touch the stone. But even as he did so a sixth sense warned. He continued the movement, accelerating it into a forward roll, then canted away, up the slope and away from the old man. He heard the vicious hiss of a force-knife passing close enough to him to be heard, close enough for Kipp to smell the ozone as the field discharged. He curled his feet, then bounded sharply to the left, heading for the sparse protection of a granite outcrop above the old man's camp.

But the thief was not sitting still. With one movement he had hurled the knife then risen to finish the intruder. Had the force-knife felled Kipp as the old man intended, his quest would have ended there and then. But his agility carried him too far, the old man pivoted, trying to outmaneuver muscles decades younger, reflexes seconds more precise. And in doing so, the old man lost his balance, stumbling over a pile of equipment at his feel. The fall should not have hampered him much but it did. He landed wrongly, bruising his thigh. He twisted in pain then jerked himself to his feet. He took one step, rolled glancingly off a loose rock, and pitched backward, tumbling down the slope toward the plain on the evening side of the ridge.

Kipp heard rather than saw the old man's fall. Breathing heavily, he glanced back at the campsite. Nothing moved. The old man was nowhere to be seen, but midway down the slope, between the crest and the blankness of the plain, an ugly fracture scarred the bleached whiteness of the ground. A bubble.

Kipp leaped out from behind the rocks. The old man might be hurt, might need help. And even if he had stolen from Kipp, he was still a human being and alone on an alien world.

The younger man flew down the slope toward the blister, his feet barely touching the loosely packed rubble.

The bubble had shattered along the entire ridge, falling in on itself. The depression was deeper than any Kipp had ever seen before, deeper and more rugged, as if the escaping gases that formed the blister had had to eat away at the rocky bones of the ridge itself in order to make their almost-escape eons before.

The old man lay at the bottom, an ugly blotch of darkness on white stones, unmoving, arms and legs twisted painfully. Kipp lowered himself over the edge, careful not to dislodge any more rocks. He slipped down the steep side of the depression, half-crawling, half-sliding until he came abreast of the old man.

A bright splash of red stained the rock on which the old man's head rested. More splashes seeped from under the broken body. Kipp laid a hand against the old man's neck. There was a pulse although barely perceptible. He hesitated to move the old man. Bones were obviously shattered, muscles torn from ligaments. The same voice, querulous, now with a hint of a whine, stuttered a few broken words. Kipp leaned closer, trying to understand them.

"…my gems…best…got me a Changer. None…none other…."

There was a harsh intake of breath, a final flutter, and all was still. Gradually the spreading pools of red ceased to spread. The old man was dead.

Kipp felt a tear starting, viciously wiped it away. He would have killed the thief if he had to. He would have. But he hadn't wanted anything like this. The pain. The suffering, even for those few moments. He had never seen anyone die, had certainly never been this responsible for a death. He could have killed in anger, he was sure, but to have to stand by and watch the life bleed away….

He struggled to his feet and began the arduous climb out of the pit. When he reached the lip he pulled himself up over the sharp edges, then moved up the slope toward the camp site.

By the time he arrived, twilight had set in. He was trapped there, much as he hated the idea. He would have to remain on the ridge until dawn.

He couldn't stand the thought of spending the night at the old man's camp, even though his own provisions lay scattered invitingly around on the bare earth. They could wait until morning, until light.

He huddled up against the rocks on the farther side of the ridge. Fortunately the night was warm, the stars bright. He did not sleep much. He spent the long hours thinking, remembering the stricken look on the old man's face, comparing that final fractional second, the fleeting glimpse of self-satisfaction, with the cunning mask that had stared over a humped shoulder at him. Why had the old man thrown the knife? For that matter, why had he thrown the Moonblood gem?

For the first time since the entire episode began, Kipp remembered the stone. It lay out there, somewhere, where he had dropped it as he had scrabbled to evade the attack. It would be there in the morning. He would find it and….

It had been a perfect stone, he could remember that much. Faintly pear-shaped, with a curious swirl of silver, almost calligraphic, suggesting interlacing initials—an *M* and a *W*, flawlessly engraved on a scarlet satin background.

As usual, Kipp woke at dawn. The sun was barely cresting the horizon as he stood stiffly, adjusted his kit on his back, and marched slowly toward the dead campsite. He avoided looking toward the blister.

Everything was there—food packets, salt pellets wrapped in their weather-impervious shells of metallic foil, flashes, everything. Kipp carefully separated his things from the old man's meager belongings, piling the latter up against one of the stones of the fire pit. When he had finished, he wrapped the battered gear in a corner of canvas torn from the old man's kit. Before he left, he would return it to its rightful owner, but not quite yet.

He straightened, scanning the rough ground. The gem should be around somewhere.

He searched. It had disappeared. Completely. Probably it had fallen into one of the small fissures that laced the ridge. Crystals lined the sides of the clefts, often only millimeters from each other. No, it was gone for good, Kipp decided dejectedly. He would have loved to get a closer look....

What, what was that? Just out of his range of vision, barely within his peripheral range, he had sensed—not actually seen, but sensed—movement. His eyes darted toward the area. Nothing. No, something. A hesitant wavering, as if the air were partially solidified.

A force-cube.

Kipp had never actually seen one, but there was no mistaking the hazy outlines of sides and top. The cube was small, only about twenty centimeters on each side, which explained how it had escaped Kipp's notice before. But it was empty. Wasn't it?

He edged closer.

No, not empty. A...thing..., a quivering ball of dust-colored fluff huddled in one corner, blending so completely with the pervasive tawny brown of Daphnis that he had to look twice to convince himself of its existence. He had never seen anything like it. As far as he knew, nothing like it was supposed to exist on the planet. Small as it was, it was far larger than the indigenous life-forms he had read about. Yet Kipp could not doubt that the creature was native. The protective coloration was keyed too truly to Daphnis for any other possibility.

The ball of fluff moved, looking up at Kipp. At least he assumed that it looked at him. He had a glimpse of what might have been deep umber eyes. Then without warning, Kipp was overwhelmed by hatred for the force-cube. His blood pounded, his pulse ran, nothing would do but that he should destroy the invisible walls that kept the creature imprisoned.

Not thinking, not even aware of the curious intensity of his desire, Kipp raced back to the camp. Somewhere in the old man's belongings he would find a small black box—he knew he would recognize it—the control box for the cube. He need only depress the third button on the left and the cube would disappear. So intense was his search that he did not pause to consider *how* he knew about the mechanisms of the cube. He only *knew*, and that was sufficient for the moment. He hoped that the old man was not carrying the control when he went over…no, here it is, stuffed in the side pocket of the thread-bare kit.

Kipp drew out the black object, fitting it comfortably into the palm of his left hand. With his right, he brushed the proper button. The box yelped and crackled once, then fell silent. Glancing over his shoulder, he could see that the cube had disappeared…and so had the ball of fluff.

He stared at the control. How had he known? And why had he pushed the buttons with the finger of his right hand? He was left-handed.

Well, at least the little thing was free. That was the important thing. Kipp hated cages and pens. After his terms of duty on spacers, his hatred had become almost phobic. Whatever the old man had trapped, the thing was free, loose, living as it should, unbothered by human interference on a planet to which humans did not belong.

Kipp slumped to the ground, drained by the intensity of his emotions, the frenzy of his search, and the relief that he had not had to search the old man's body. Let him rest there, undisturbed, a victim of his own… greed?

For the moment, Kipp was content to sit back, neck and shoulders resting roughly against a rock, legs stretched out languidly, hands trailing along the ground. His left hand began moving, unconsciously, fingering the smooth facets of a crystal shard, rubbing the surfaces.

Almost without warning, his flexing fingers bushed against a satiny warmth. Kipp looked down. The fluffy thing lay quietly between his extended arm and his side. It was motionless. Up close, he could vaguely detect what appeared to be legs—four, or perhaps two legs and two manipulative limbs, analogous to arms but doubling as supports when the creature was at rest. The head was large for the rest of the body, with a rounded snout ending in small but sharp-looking teeth. The thing nearly resembled a large, unusually furry hamster, except that it was far more fragilely constructed, more ethereal, more alien—as it should look, Kipp reminded himself. This was not earth; this was Daphnis, the unknown, the untamed. He tensed unconsciously, only to feel an immediate sense of warmth and well-being. He could not bring himself to fear the little thing, regardless of his total ignorance of what it was, whether it was dangerous or not, where it came from, and why it had nestled onto the ground next to him.

He reached out slowly with his hand, palm outward, and brushed the tawny fur with the back of his hand. The creature did not flinch; in fact, Kipp would have sworn that it returned the gesture, turning it into almost a caress. And simultaneously, Kipp was flooded by an ungovernable sense of trust and...well, he could only define it as *love*.

He straightened. Those weren't his emotions. He had no reason to love and trust the alien thing huddling beside him. No reason at all, unless....

Telepathy?

No, that was patently absurd. He had heard no voices, had not felt any words form within his brain.

Empathy, then?

Perhaps. An outpouring of emotional empathy, stemming from the creature and directed toward himself.

He looked down at the ball of fluff. Even as he did so, he felt a flowing of acceptance, of affirmation.

"Well, I'll be...." Kipp grinned gleefully, reveling in the knowledge that he had been accepted by...the thing. Whatever it was, it trusted him, it wanted him to join with it.

"Friends, right?" Kipp felt no uncertainly about speaking out loud. Forming the words and verbalizing them seemed to intensify the emotional content of his communication. Again he felt the unmistakable assent emanating from the thing.

He opened his hand, allowing the tiny creature to climb up onto his palm. Slowly, carefully he raised his hand until the fluff-ball was close to his face. His breath stirred the dusky fur. From this distance, he could see the two bright eyes clearly. He raised the other hand, stroked the fur, surprised by its fineness and smoothness. The thing must be ninety percent fur; dripping wet, it would probably be nothing more than two sets of match-stick limbs, connected by a fifth short stick, with a knobby skull at one end. There was no tail.

Kipp sat for a long while, murmuring sibilants to the creature, enjoying the backwash of emotions from it. He felt needed, wanted, appreciated—and all because he had canceled out the force-cube in which the old man had kept the thing imprisoned. He would have done it anyway, but he enjoyed his reward.

Finally, though, the warmth of the angling sun grew too much to sit idly. He leaned over and set the creature on the ground, and was startled to discover that it all but disappeared. The protective coloration was absolute. When motionless, as it was now, the thing would be able to disappear at will, as if invisible.

"You better watch out, critter. I might step on you by accident, and I wouldn't want that." Kipp felt sure the creature had sent assurance back to him.

He moved carefully to one side, well away from where he had been sitting, then began collecting and packing his possessions. He had to get going. He needed to find that last, perfect stone, the one that would get him off Daphnis and back into civilization.

He straightened dismally. And, he reminded himself, he had to bury the old man.

The job did not take long, although it was both distasteful and arduous. He decided to leave the body where it had landed, in the bowl of the depression, surrounded by the crusted blood. He felt the body of the old man's coat cursorily, then backed away. There was no evidence of anything, no identification papers, passes, anything like that. Quickly Kipp gathered the largest nearby rocks and built a cairn over the body. Then he clambered out of the pit and slung the old man's kit over his shoulder. Climbing back down was more difficult with the additional weight, but he made it safely to the bottom. He set the kit near the head of the make-shift grave, then carefully layered smaller stones over it. There was no need to fear predators or scavengers on Daphnis, but he felt the urgency of providing this last service for a fellow-human, even if a thief, a liar, and a would-be murderer. The old man had probably been half-crazy anyway, from loneliness, privation, and age. Kipp really couldn't find it in himself to blame the old fellow. If only he hadn't thrown that knife....

For the third time, Kipp struggled up the loosely

packed slope of the blister, to stand balanced on the knife-edge just long enough to survey his handiwork. There was no trace of the body; still, Kipp felt that he would recognize the place again. If need be, he would try to lead a party back from the port to recover the body.

Rubbing his scraped and blistered hands on the rough seams of his trousers, he headed up-slope toward his own kit. Back to work, he thought, got to get cracking if I'm going to find that big one.

His hand was almost touching the webbing of his kit when he saw the ball of fluff perched on the edge of the kit as if waiting for him.

He laughed. The sound echoed through the wastes, brightening the day, flooding over the plains below. The release was spontaneous and ecstatic.

He bent down and scooped up the creature, petting it as he did so.

"What brings you back here? I though you would be long gone, back to your home, wherever it is. Although you are welcome to join me if you want."

He couldn't help himself. The warm tones of wistfulness filtered through his voice, communicating Kipp's need to the tiny creature. In response, Kipp felt it huddle down in his palm, content and secure.

"Okay, traveling companions it is. But what to call you. I can't just say 'thing' every time I want to talk to you." He leaned against a nearby rock. Mentally he worked through lists of hypothetical names: pet names, people names, outlandish names, exotic names, alien names. Nothing suited.

Finally he re-considered. This was Daphnis, wasn't it? And this twitching bit of life belonged here, didn't it. Okay then: "How about *Daphna*?"

The creature seemed to consider the suggestion. Without warning, Kipp was overwhelmed against by the strong emotional output of the creature. She approved, of that there could be no doubt. And she *was* female. Kipp had not even considered that consciously in selecting a name.

"Okay, Daphna. Let's get going."

Even as he began moving , she slipped between his fingers and tumbled nearly his full height to the sharply faceted rocks at his feet. He bit his lip, fearful that she might have been injured, but she landed with almost feline confidence, bounding off before she had stopped falling. He could follow her movements, but only with the utmost concentration. At times she seemed more a blur against the background than anything else.

Finally she stopped, nosing into a narrow crack between two rocks. Kipp called to her without any effect. He could sense her excitement, her eagerness to get something for him, to show him something. So he stepped over to the crack. She backed away, her front paws closed as if in prayer. Kipp could barely restrain himself from laughing, she looked so smug, so self-satisfied.

He glanced into the crack but could see nothing. Her interest intensified. He knelt down, peering into the darkness. Nothing.

Still, she urged him. Finally he stretched out prone on the sharp rocks, his nose nearly in the crack.

And there it was. A vagrant beam of light flickered off the scarlet of the Moonblood gem.

Kipp flushed with excitement and frustration. So close—less than twenty centimeters away lay the fortune he was searching for—but there was no way he could get to it. He jammed his hand into the crack, oblivious to the ripping and tearing against his flesh. His fingers stretched until he felt like the bones would split his fingertips. But not enough. He jerked his kit from his shoulders, running through his equipment, trying first one thing, then another. Nothing reached. He sat back, exhausted. Daphna had not moved the entire time.

He looked over at her and grinned.

"Thanks, old girl, but I just can't get to it. If I had some digging equipment, maybe, but I don't. It'll just have to rest in there forever. I saw it though. I held it in my hand. That is something, at any rate."

As he hunched over to catch his breath, she flooded him with sorrow, pity, and understanding—then raced off toward the crest of the ridge.

When she returned, she cradled a crystal in her fore-paws...in her hands, Kipp decided. She held the crystal out to him. It was large, flawless, with intricate strands of silver threading through it. But it was white.

He shook his head sadly. "Sorry, this one won't do. Wrong color. But thanks, anyway."

He let the crystal slip through his fingers. Daphna

scurried over and retrieved it. For a moment Kipp thought that she was trying to eat it. She struggled with the bulk, forcing it, not into her mouth, as he had originally thought, but into a pouch under her chin, almost as if she were a kangaroo with an over-sized offspring. She nudged and prodded at the recalcitrant lump until satisfied with its position. Kipp laughed. Now she looked like an off-centered, lopsided mop head. She squealed her disapproval of the image.

He scooped her up in his hands and settled her securely on the shoulder of his jacket.

"Let's get going, lady. We've got work ahead of us."

She chattered approvingly as he set out, his long legs easily working into a comfortable, swinging rhythm.

The day passed uneventfully. They crossed one of the plain-basins, barren stretched unbroken by any hint of vegetation. Only the ever-pervasive streamlets cut through the uninterrupted vistas. They made good time; in terrain of this sort, it was useless to search for any gems. There were not even any white crystals scattered on the even ground. By late afternoon, they had successfully crossed, having avoided several potential blisters but meeting with few other difficulties.

As evening drew on, Kipp and Daphna emerged from the flatlands to a new area of low ridges—and behind them the single line of near-mountains that Kipp had seen in the distance the day before. Perhaps there the chances of finding gems might improve.

He had talked to Daphna throughout the day of himself, his past, his hopes, his plans. And she had understood. He was convinced of that. True, they had not discovered any way of communicating directly through words, but he could sense occasional emotional washes from her. He had talked of his childhood, of his mother's sacrifices to pay for his education that had opened the stars to him, and he was positive that the tiny creature had not only understood but had reflected his own images of his mother, images of warmth and comfort and generation—only amplified and weirdly distorted. Still recognizable, but different in ways that Kipp could not quite define.

Hour by hour he had talked, pouring himself into Daphna, allowing her to respond to his emotional intensities. Until finally, by the time they left the plain, he felt closer to the furry ball than to…well, than to anyone living he could name. They shared completely, empathically. In large measure, they were one.

They made camp that evening—a dry camp, along the lower edge of the line of ridges—and both human and Daphnidian fell immediately asleep. They were exhausted, both from the incessant walking and from the exchanges that had taken place. During the night, Kipp dreamed, something unusual for him. When he woke the next dawn, he could not remember details but the dreams had been soothing and restful. He stood and stretched, noticing the pleasurable lack of stiffness or knots. He was ready to face a new day.

Daphna was also. She scurried around the encampment, her dusty fur quivering in excitement. So far, however, she had masked her emotions sufficiently that Kipp had no inkling of their cause.

He squatted to pick at a packet of dry food. He didn't feel like going to the trouble of cooking. He wasn't really hungry, come to think of it, though the travels of the previous day should have made him ravenous. He looked about, spotting Daphna near an outcrop of rocks. He was getting better at locating her. She no longer looked quite so much like a wisp of dust flitting just beyond his circle of vision.

"Daphna, here!"

She jerked her head, looking back at him with a quizzically wise expression.

"Food." He mumbled a fragment of protein from the package, then held it invitingly between outstretched fingers. She scrambled toward him, wrinkled her nose three or four times at the morsel, then jumped on his wrist and climbed to her perch on his shoulder.

"Not hungry, eh?" He laughed. Then he sobered. He had never seen her eat. She had eaten nothing all yesterday, nor the evening before as far as he knew. Nor had she left him during the night, he thought.

She must eat something, he worried. Then he corrected himself. Why? After all, this was not Earth. Why should she conform to life forms native to a planet that was to her alien and impossibly distant. In fact, according to everything he had read, she shouldn't even exist on *this* planet.

But she did. He laughed again as he fine fur tickled the outer edge of his ear.

Daphna sat still for a few seconds, then began

tugging and pulling at something. He could feel her hind paws digging into his jacket as she wrestled and prodded.

Then suddenly as a cut from a force-knife, a thin wailing pierced the air—and Kipp was overpowered by intense feelings of fear and despair.

He swiveled his head, careful not to disturb her hold. She was grasping the crystal between outstretched forepaws, as if offering it to him. He started to reach for it, then stopped.

It flamed scarlet.

A Moonblood gem.

Yet it was the same crystal she had secreted in her pouch the morning after he had rescued her. He recognized the intertwining filaments of silver, now flaming on a crimson back drop.

At the same time, he felt a chill spreading through his body. His muscles froze, his bone felt brittle and frail. He felt—*knew* himself in some arcane manner to be—centuries old.

He stared at his hand. It was smooth, unlined and young, unmarked, except for the scar along his thumb, a souvenir of a childhood accident. It was his hand, yet he seemed to see it from a different perspective. It appeared large, inexplicably alien.

Daphna!

She was no longer projecting amorphous emotional states; she was giving him an image, showing him what she saw from her point of view. He stood up, seeing herself in his mind, elongated, ill-proportioned, but essentially human.

Then that vision faded, replaced by another. In this view, he had aged, aged beyond belief. His youthful body was wrinkled and crooked, bent, twisted, wasted with years, decades, centuries.

And then it passed. He was himself again.

Somehow, he realized that Daphna was telling him, not about himself, about his own future, but about hers. She was dying. The crystal had blossomed crimson overnight, and with that blossoming, Daphna had changed.

Changed.

A *changer*! Kipp felt he was on the verse of discovering something crucial, when Daphna interrupted, incessantly tugging at his consciousness. He turned his thoughts to her.

She was pleading with him. He felt her impelling him toward the top of the ridge, and from there along an unseen pathway. He looked up. Beyond, the mountains loomed, larger than Kipp would have imagined possible on Daphnis' eternal flatness.

"There?" He pointed. From her perch on his shoulder, Daphna quivered violently. There could be no mistaking the positiveness of her response. She needed to reach those mountains—and in her present state, Kipp realized, she could not cover half the distance before she would be dead.

"Up we go, then."

During most of the march, Daphna remained silent and still. She rarely intruded into Kipp's consciousness…and Kipp felt the loss. There for a few moments at the camp site, they had drawn closer. Kipp was certain that they could communicate now, not just in shared emotions but in exchanged images—speak, in a non-verbal sense. He tried once to rouse Daphna but could feel the extreme effort the exchange cost her. So he refrained. He kept up a running monologue, as much for his own benefit as for hers, while continuously running his fingers along the smooth facets of the Moonblood gem in his pocket. She had given it to him. He had taken her offering, although he did not yet understand its importance or its meaning.

By evening they had again crossed a plain and were now in real foothills. The slopes were more angular, with fewer cracks and practically no crystals at all. Daphna was becoming erratically excitable; she would chatter and quiver for long moments, then subside into a coma-like state. Kipp cursed his lack on knowledge about the indigenous life of Daphnis, then reminded himself that he probably already knew more about Daphna and her kind than anyone else, and that was precious little. If only he could help her.

She showed no interest in food. If anything, his crumbles of protein repulsed her. Nor would she drink. Kipp could not believe that any creature could exist on nothingness, yet that seemed to be the case.

During her periods of excitement, Kipp could occasionally catch enough seepage through her control to know that they were heading in the right direction. She was increasingly active for longer periods, although even that worried Kipp. She seemed to be burning herself out, using up what reserves she had. Again and again, his fingers rubbed against the flaming fury of the gem in his pocket, as if trying to will part of its energy, its violent inner life, into Daphna.

Just before twilight, she roused herself from a longer than usual period of somnolence. And she roused more in control than she had been before. She straightened, gripping into the fabric of Kipp's jacket with her hind paws, steadying herself by lightly brushing a forepaw against his ear. He barely noticed the tickling. She was looking for a landmark, a sign, something.

He stopped, scarcely breathing in his empathic bond with her.

The search, long and careful, almost despairing.

Then the discovery, sudden and sure.

As one being, human and Daphnidian scrambled up the left-hand slope, struggling to reach the shadowed mouth of a cave before night should fall completely and blend the spot of blackness into the surrounding blackness of the slope. They had to reach it soon. Kipp felt that Daphna would not survive the night in the open. She had to reach that cave.

And they did. His fingers were raw and bleeding in a dozen places, his pants ripped along one knee where he had scraped against the edge of a broken blister as the rim had given way beneath him…he had become careless in his haste. The climb could not have taken more than fifteen minutes, yet it had seemed to stretch eternally. The longer they climbed, the farther away the wavering spot of blackness seemed. And Daphna was slipping from him, literally and figuratively. He finally had to reach over with one hand and lift her off his shoulder. He placed her in the outer pouch of his jacket, near his heart, where he could protect her with his shoulders.

But they made it. Just as the last sliver of sun had disappeared, just as the final glimmer of light faded, they entered the cave.

The darkness was more compelling than any he had ever experienced. With one hand, he loosened the flap on the jacket pouch, allowing Daphna to crawl back up onto his shoulder. She seemed paradoxically stronger and frailer. He could see nothing but found himself picking a careful trail through the depths of the cavern, descending into the entrails of the mountain itself. He walked carefully but surely, blinded but confident as each step drew him nearer to....

In his pocket, the Moonblood rested, his fingers still caressing it.

On an impulse he withdrew it from his pocket. The stone glowed in the darkness, evilly it seemed to him altnough he could not define why. Daphna started at the intrusion of the light, then quivered uncontrollably. He jammed the stone back into his pocket.

Finally, after who knew how long walking in darkness, he slowed, rubbing his blinded eyes with an invisible hand. He blinked several times, glanced down toward the unseen path, then raised his eye.

There was no mistake. Ahead, the cavern was

touched with a faint glow. He moved ahead, more quickly now, with less care. Soon the hint of a glow became a gleam, growing brighter and brighter with each step, burning with ever-increasing power.

Daphna was virtually comatose now. She had long since ceased moving at all, and for the past few minutes had stopped the chirruping whisper that had accompanied Kipp through the darkness. He had to hurry.

The glow increased, but even so he was not prepared for the sudden brilliance as he rounded one final corner.

It was as if he had been trapped within the heart of a Moonblood gem itself.

He was in a large cave, its sides and roof receding beyond his vision. All around—on every side, above, below, beneath the dusty tread of his boots—the cavern glowed. Silver threads coruscated in their combined radiance, lancing through shadowed corners, behind incipient stalactites, whirling and rushing as if in perpetual movement. Behind them, less scintillating, more subdued, yet more terrifyingly vital and vivid, the blood-red undercurrents buoyed the silver filaments. Where before, in the darkness of the tunnel, the light of a single stone had seemed malevolent, vicious, evil, this riotous symphony of light filled Kipp with wonder and delight...until he saw it.

At first he did not notice the spot of darkness near the center of the cavern. His eyes were bedazzled, his mind befuddled by the intensity of the light. Then the darkness moved, drawing his attention irrevocably toward itself.

There, in the middle of life—of vibrance, of fire, warmth, and power—he faced death. He drew in his breath, expelled it violently. Suddenly the air felt tainted, stale, decaying. The fiery walls, floor, ceiling did not fade, but the darkness within them deepened, overwhelmed them, consumed them.

Slowly the spot of darkness drew closer, until he could define the shape.

Daphna.

No, that was absurd. She was still on his shoulder, her tiny paws gripping the seam of his jacket, coldly, convulsively, deftly. He could feel the breath of weight he had always felt. No this…this thing was not Daphna.

It was too large, he now realized. It was bloated and dark, nearly hairless, covered with wrinkles and chafing, as if its skin hung too loosely and abraded itself against its own roughness. Great spots of cancerous growths hung laxly upon the thing's flanks. Daphna had always seemed an exhalation of springtime breath, light, frivolous, and airy. This gargantuan parody of her was heavy, earth-bound…yet of her own kind.

Kipp's eyes filled with tears. This monstrosity was one with Daphna in a way that he could never be… and it wanted her. He felt no emotional contact with the thing, perceived no images, certainly heard no commanding words, yet he found himself leaning down, placing the still form on the pulsing floor, and watching silently, dispassionately as the darkness rolled toward it, surrounded it, engulfed it, and retreated. When he looked again, the floor was bare;

near the farthest wall, the darkness huddled.

A soft crooning filled the chamber, bringing with it a hint of fresh air, of breezes along the many rivulets of Daphnis. The gemstone walls and ceiling roared their cold fires, scarlet and silver, until the two merged. In his last moments of consciousness, Kipp was certain that the darkness opposing him had suddenly burst into flame, radiating unbearably through the overpowering cavern.

Slowly, as if he were a puppet gently lowered to rest, Kipp slid to the floor, his head resting on a curling intaglio of silver cut with blood.

He awoke at dawn as usual. He lay for a moment, eyes closed, savoring the subtle odors of morning. He started to stretch, then froze.

Daphna.

His eyes flew open, already studying his surroundings. He recognized the slope. He was just below the cave entrance, where they had been last night when Daphna had discovered her goal. He raised one hand to shade his eyes as he surveyed the mountainside for the black opening.

He looked at his hand. The cuts were healed. He could see hairline scars where they had been. Already the scars seemed fainter, as if they would soon disappear completely, leaving his hands unmarked. He glanced down. His pants were still ripped, but the abrasion on his knee had faded.

He looked back toward the summit of the mountain.

The cave had disappeared.

Perhaps the whole incredible episode had been merely a dream. Perhaps he had only thought he had scraped himself as he had flailed his unprotected hands against the stony ground, caught in the web of a nightmare. Perhaps....

But no. No perhaps. It had been true.

Out of the corner of his eye, he caught a fleeting glimpse of a movement, a distortion of the rocks, as if shimmering heat waves danced before it. But the air was still too cool.

Daphna.

He stood still, afraid to move, afraid that she would not remember him. She was even more ethereal than she had been the first time he saw her. Her fur was sublimated into virtual invisibility, here eyes merely two glinting sparks reflecting from a hidden crystal in the rock. She was Daphna—that much he knew. Yet she was...different. More part of Daphnis again, less part of him.

He remained motionless, but his lips parted as he whispered her name, breathing out the final vowel as if in hopes that the sound would never have to end.

"Daphna."

He half expected to hear an answering voice. He could almost hear its fragile loveliness, its airiness. But instead he felt the familiar wash of approbation, merging with...understanding.

He was not consciously aware of how, but suddenly he knew what had happened in the cave. That...thing, that grotesque mockery of Daphna had once been like

Daphna herself. There were only a handful of them left on the planet now, the generative forces out of which Daphna and her few sisters had sprung ages before—the mothers, if you will, of Daphna's race. They had chosen the darkness, the ugliness, the ageless death of the caves, in order that their children might exist. Daphna had not eaten since Kipp had found her; she would in fact never eat. She existed on the radiance, the radiation (to use a colder but probably more precise term) that the mother-things exuded—and that transformed the white crystals of Daphnis into Moonblood gems.

Daphna was a Changer. She had been dying, her vitality drained—perhaps by the old man, who had apparently imprisoned her until, in her final moments, she would alter the lacteal crystals into gems, dying to create unutterable beauty. Or perhaps merely by encroaching age.

Age.

Kipp could feel the press of years, of centuries. Daphna and her kind must be essentially immortal, so long as they could reach the mother-forces in time to enter into the darkness and death and emerge young, fresh, newly alive. Eventually, Daphna would make her own choice. She would immure herself within the hollowness of the mountains, sealing herself in darkness. And from that darkness would emerge a few more of her kind—her children, as like her now as twins, as unlike what she would willingly become as night and day.

The wash of understanding receded. Kipp breathed again. He blinked against the sunlight. When he could see again, the shimmering had disappeared. Daphna was gone.

He dug his hand into his pocket, clutching smoothness, pulling it out.

In the morning light the Moonblood gem was flawless, pure, and infinitely beautiful. It had come from darkness, from darkness and death, but it was absolute in its integral beauty. A legacy from Daphnis.

He placed it carefully in his leather pouch, next to the pitiful few fragments he had already found. Perhaps they would be enough for his fare off this world. He wouldn't have to part with the stone, with Daphna.

As he turned to descend the mountain's shoulder, he caught a final, hesitant glimpse of a tawny shimmering on a ledge above. He saluted the emptiness, then walked away.

He was a young man. In the presence of the agelessness of youth on Daphnis, he felt old, tired, and word.

His hand felt again for the smoothness. His shoulders straightened.

"Good-bye, Daphna," he whispered.

AMBASSADOR

The boy wandered through the park, kicking piles of dry leaves and muttering to himself. When he came upon the lone, gigantic oak standing in the exact center of the park, he threw himself to the ground beneath it, glad for the momentary shade and for the feeling of cool grass against his hot cheek. Even now, nearly an hour later, the blood still pounded at his temples and his cheeks flushed scarlet.

She did that to him every time.

Every damned time.

Like he was just a kid or something.

He crooked one arm and buried his eyes in welcome darkness, breathing green freshness from the crushed blades of grass. A diligent watcher in the thick leaves above might possibly have noticed a tremor beneath the thin T-shirt, a sob swallowed before it came fully to life. Or perhaps not. After all, the boy *was* too old to cry.

* * * * *

The final stages of phasis still lingered. FairSpeaker shook convulsively, bristling his thick pelt as excess charges drained away. His vision remained slightly blurred, but he could nonetheless easily define the major throughways among the City's chlorophyllous structures. OneRuler had done well, as always, setting him down right on target. He was megaLeaps from the frightening wilderness of heaped-up stone and alien brightness surrounding the City.

FairSpeaker blinked rapidly, clearing his sight. Ah yes...this City was fair, even if strangely silent. Not a sentient in sight, unless....

He leaned cautiously outward, gripping tightly to the spongy tissue beneath him.

Unless perhaps that creature below was a sentient native. Of course, it looked too massive, too inert, too cumbersomely bulky to have attained sentience (*the Inverse Law of Mentality*, he reminded himself), but then this *was* an alien world. Physical laws might differ slightly, even physiological ones, for that matter. This was, after all, far out in one of the distant arms of the MilkCircle.

And the creature *had* already assumed the appropriate posture of obeisance. That if nothing else must attest to its superior mental levels.

FairSpeaker drew himself up, aware of the Cosmic Significance of this moment. Every Word would be beamed instantaneously to OneRuler, but FairSpeaker knew himself to be ready, more than sufficient for the task at hand. He had practiced the precise wording, the exact intonational nuances. Even transmitted through alien air to alien ears, the intent—if not precisely the content—of the message should succeed.

He ducked his head in the requisite jerky bow, just once as protocol demanded, and began to speak….

* * * * *

It took several moments for the boy to notice the sound, the single break in the general silence. It sounded like a squirrel—a high chittering, musical and oddly pleasant. For a few seconds, he lay there, cheek against the bruised grass, enjoying the sound, forgetting (almost) the measured cruelty of her last words.

And then forgetting entirely. The sound teased at him, becoming almost like words that fading again into music. He raised himself on one elbow and looked around.

Nothing.

He raised his eyes, shading them against the shards of light refracted by the leaf-cover.

Nothing. No, wait—there, on that branch. He squinted, trying harder to focus on the vaguely defined shape. For some reason, it seemed more diffuse than he expected, more a mere outline against green shadow than a thing of substance and weight. A trick of the light, he decided.

But it was definitely the source of the sound. The boy sat upright and cocked his head to one side, listening.

* * * * *

Excellent, FairSpeaker thought as he continued his

introductory remarks. The creature had assumed the posture of attention, as was appropriate. OneRuler would be pleased, if for no other reason than that the native's actions had thus substantiated OneRuler's dictates on the universality of communication signals. FairSpeaker could almost imagine OneRuler lecturing to the Schoolers, chiding them for their wild fears and warnings.

As if all sentients did not share the universal languages of body, sound, and space. Indeed!

Excited—but masking his excitement beneath the steady pacing of his message—FairSpeaker continued, launching into his perfunctory history of OneWorld, that distant diadem that lay glittering beyond the far arc of this MilkCircle.

* * * * *

The boy listened for another moment or two.

You know, it really did sound like that squirrel was giving a speech or something. Looked like it, too. It balanced upright on its haunches, its fur fluffed pompously around its neck. And there were almost lilts in the chatter, like pauses, rhythms.

The boy shaded his eyes and squinted again. He couldn't quite see the forepaws, but they seemed to be moving back and forth, like a preacher's hands gesturing at the pulpit. It was funny.

He straightened up. "Che-che-che," he chattered, grinning broadly.

* * * * *

FairSpeaker froze.

His tender green imaginings of power and prestige abruptly twisted and browned. If only there were some way to stop the transmission, to edit the record!

Beneath his russet pelt, he paled and his verdant blood chilled.

What had he done to incense the creature so? He had only been listing the major artistic achievements of the People over the past lifetime of circuits—certainly innocent enough, void of any political ramifications. *Why then had the creature risen in anger/fear and spewed out that obscene distortion of that archaic, atavistic BattleCry?*

FairSpeaker was deeply shaken...but he was no coward. He braced himself, pulled himself to his full and not insubstantial height, and began to speak again. But when he looked down and saw the impossibly thin lips opening to reveal huge rows of equally huge white teeth bared in the rictus of challenge, even he nearly fainted.

* * * * *

The squirrel had abruptly stopped chittering. The boy rocked back on his heels, as quietly as possible. He had startled it, scared it into silence...just like she did to him, just like girls always did. No matter how hard he tried, he always managed to say something stupid and insulted them. He was doomed to be a sexless hermit forever.

If only he could figure out what to say to her, how to explain and apologize without making things worse. But his fifteen years—almost sixteen, really—had not included any experiences that promised to help him out of the mess he had made this time.

He slumped back to the matted grass. For a while he didn't even listen for the squirrel.

* * * * *

When all is lost, at least keep up appearances, FairSpeaker reminded himself sternly.

He began again, cautiously, from the beginning, watching the creature carefully for any physiologically transmitted signals of anger. He had to make amends, somehow, to mollify the creature, persuade it back into a pleasant, open frame of mind.

He performed fluently for several sentences. There were no signs of anger now, no threats…only the self-effacement of apology and humility.

Excellent.

Now for that difficult passage.

He began the next part of his message, extemporaneously abbreviating the account of OneWorld's culture sufficient to slip over the disastrous statements on Art. At least he hoped he had.

A quick glance downward.

No antagonistic responses. *Fine. Wonderful.* Now on to the real issue—the invitation to join OneWorld in a unity of trade and exchange.

* * * * *

The boy looked up. The squirrel was still there, apparently over its moment of fright—probably too dumb to remember that it had even *been* frightened— and was chattering on. The sounds insinuated themselves through his depression again, cheering and somehow even inspiring him.

Slowly, so slowly as to seem unmoving, he straightened, stood, raised one outstretched hand toward the branch above him. The squirrel didn't seem to notice. The boy ventured to take a step. Closer, the boy noticed that the squirrel still seemed rather soft and hazy, with fur so fine that it disappeared at the edges.

It saw him and stopped chattering. It seemed to melt into the shadows, and then abruptly it was back again, silent and still.

The boy waited for a few seconds before he dared to make any sounds. "Hi fella. Pretty fella. Pretty, pretty, pretty…." He wasn't really speaking, not consciously, just making marginally vocalized purr-noises. The sounds were all he wanted, all he needed. He didn't want to frighten the poor little thing again.

* * * * *

FairSpeaker listened with mounting horror. He did not move, as he had been commanded. He had lost control for just a breath and had begun to fade into phasis, but then he forced himself to stop. To retreat would have been too obvious, too open an admission of defeat. He still lived, his hearts still beat—there was hope yet that he might pacify this barbarian and wrench victory out of defeat. And no creature could move fast enough to capture one of the People, especially one with phasis-augmentation. Physically, at least, he was safe.

But the language...the utter—the unutterable—depravity of the words spilling from this...this *thing*. FairSpeaker blushed in vicarious shame for all sentients, if a sentient-shape could debase itself like this. True, FairSpeaker was incapable of understanding each individual sound-packet, but the ideas they so blatantly communicated were clear and explicit.

Suddenly, he could control himself no longer. The creature might be gigantic, this planet monstrous beyond all dimension, the situation fraught with potential disaster for at least two star systems...but he was, after all, only human. Surely not even OneRuler would expect him to sit back and take this...this *filth,* this undeserved tirade, this abomination.

Eyes glittering, FairSpeaker began fervently, summoning forth a fury that defied his own name. *FairSpeaker* no more! but *TruthTeller.* He aimed his words like darts downward toward the creature beneath him. The creature's flaring pinkish ears would flame at what they were about to receive from him!

* * * * *

The squirrel sang again, high-pitched and rapid,

comical sounds that lightened the heaviness in the boy's heart—or, truth be told, somewhere nearer his stomach. The boy dropped his hand, again slowly, hoping not to disturb the little thing in its song. He listened, almost forgetting his cares.

* * * * *

It had responded, TruthTeller noted obliquely. It had withdrawn its rough appendage from his own private and personal space, a proxemic apology (at least the beginnings of one) for its barbarous behavior. It was a sufficient beginning...but no more. He continued his harangue, caught up in his own anger and the power of his unassailable rhetoric.

* * * * *

The little thing seemed to be getting carried away. Its thin, high whistles and spits had blurred into a constant stream of sound. And it way it perched on that branch, ears pricking up and paws folded against its belly, its tail raised like a pennant—it looked for all the world as if it were scolding him for interfering with its search for a left-over nut from last season.

Cute!

The boy laughed, long, loud and uproarious laughter that cleared his mind. He laughed until he cried and his stomach began hurting, that irritating pseudo-pain that only intensified his laughter.

But finally he stopped and lay still, prone on the

grass. He looked up. The squirrel was gone.

* * * * *

The explosion shook TruthTeller, physically and psychically. The creature had turned in an instant from threat to open violence! TruthTeller's ears, sensitive as they were to the slightest subtleties of sound, had been nearly deafened by that first volley of waves—oh! the unbelievable pain. And from the mouth of a sentient!

TruthTeller fell down and crouched on all fours, instinctively seeking the universal posture of capitulation. Only gradually did the political implications of that single action filter through his mind. Through his cowardice he had irrevocably compromised the status—perhaps even the sovereignty—of OneWorld and OneRuler. He had capitulated before the barrage of a savage that was now revealed to be fully as irrational as it was hideous.

TruthTeller raised his head for a glimpse. The creature fired again, and again, and again, deafening claps of vibrations that shook the very thoroughfare that TruthTeller huddled on.

He bristled, now furious in spite of his deafness, in spite of the ringing that threatened to split his brain, in spite of his pain. The creature had ignored the signal of surrender! It continued its attacks, therefore— TruthTeller realized with a swirl of wonder—therefore and thereby invalidating TruthTeller's *own* surrender.

He raised himself to two legs, gestured sharply once, as if severing a tightly knotted cord, and hissed: "The

World is hereby interdicted. You have no decency, no civility, and no honor. Wherever we of OneWorld travel, beyond the narrow limits of this unremarkable MilkCircle, we shall spread the infamy of this place. None shall enter this space; none shall trade; none shall share ideas and progress; none, none, none! You shall remain forever backward and ignorant, the savages in truth that you are! Forever!"

The final curse shrilled into silence. TruthTeller shivered at the severity of the punishment he had inflicted upon this world, but the Words had been spoken and could not be recalled. They had been, just possibly, overly harsh. He looked down. The creature seemed to be coming to some vestige of sense. It was pulling its lower appendages upward as if in pain, as if feeling an intensity of remorse and repentance. It writhed, vibrated, as if….

This time, the explosion instantly triggered TruthTeller's automatic phasis impulse. He felt the charges surging through every cell of his body. He had just a heartsbeat to shake his head—no, he had not been wrong, not been overly harsh. Such creatures constituted a menace to all sentient life. He shimmered and disappeared, as volley after volley of devastation sped toward him. This place would remain shut off… forever.

* * * * *

The boy stood slowly, one hand clutching a painful stitch in his side, the other wiping tears from both eyes. But the laughing fit seemed finally over. Healthy laughter, healing laughter it had been, but it was over.

He glanced up at the branch. The squirrel was gone. He had probably frightened it back into its nest with his laughter. He was sorry, but honestly, it had looked so funny sitting there, acting for all the world as if it were scolding him. The memory brought a smile.

He started back across the grass toward the ring of high-rises that circled the park. As he tucked in an arrant shirttail, he thought, *I'll never understand girls. As far as I'm concerned, they might as well be from another planet.*

Then he remembered her smile, her eyes, the incredible sight of sunshine glinting off the highlights in her hair.

He almost skipped the next step or two.

Oh well, I can always try again.

THE GRAVE'S A FINELY
PRIMATE SPACE

We've had it wrong, you know, all these years. Backwards, really. And we never caught on.

I only found out by accident. I was actually heading to the cemetery for a plot.

Cemetery, hah! *Forest Lawn*—where they haven't got the first and the second is mottled with bits of concrete like a teenager's acne gone wild. But that was where they told me to go.

For a plot, that is.

Since the old man who used to shovel dirt was replaced by a machine, he makes his living selling plots. The management lets him hang around the stones, for old time's sake I suppose, so he's hard to trace. But he peddles the best plots in town, doling them out to budding writers. Rumor has it that he reads the headstones and invents stories to go with the names.

So I headed to Forest Lawn—the big one, the one that crouches like fate over Glendale, with the great mausoleum sticking up over the crest of the hill, a slab of granite giving God the finger as it hides death in almost-naked Davids topped with prurient fig leaves, and naked Graces dancing Poesque through the aisles of the dead.

I had to walk—or wanted to, I don't know which. But whichever, death hung over me. Everywhere I turned, there it was.

It had rained that spring, torrents of dirty, acidic water. Rivers backed up into sewers and the muck spilled out onto cracked pavements. Then it turned hot. And the mosquitoes came, and the frogs—two of a decalogue of plagues. The frogs weren't much of a plague, though...too dumb. They hopped around until they got squished beneath the tiger paws on the Cadillacs and Jaguars and Beemers that haunt the LA canyons. That afternoon I counted them, the dead, squished frogs. The mile walk averaged about five per dozen paces...flat, dried-up frog bodies that looked like misshapen and abandoned froggish frisbees.

I even tried one. Scraped it up and flipped it leg for leg and watched it sail over a hedge and land in a bowl of salad set out for someone's backyard barbeque.

Oh well, that's life.

And the rabbit.... I knew it had been there the day before, crushed against the asphalt, brains bubbling out and ears still twitching in the wind as a huge stink-bug trundled by. Those ears—I would have sworn they moved by themselves, as if the ears were still somehow alive and the rabbit cold-stone dead.

But the next morning it was gone. Rabbit...ears...not even a stain on the pavement to mark their passing.

It took a while that day, but I finally found the old

man. He squatted on the edge of a squarish tombstone like a cormorant, or like Fate itself.

"Plot?" he said, his voice quivering. "You want a plot? I'll *give* you plot!"

"No, you've got it wrong," I cried. "I want to *buy*...."

"Yer all the same, ya know. *Buy* this 'n' *buy* that. Nobody works, nobody thinks, nobody notices. Lord love ya...."

It seemed an odd thing for him to say, considering his position. He was squatting not quite obscenely over Mrs. Mabel Truegood, R.I.P., Beloved Mother and Devoted Wife. I thought abruptly of Evelyn Waugh's Aimee Thanatogenos—"Your little Aimee is wagging her tail in heaven"—and shuddered.

"Lord love ya" he continued, "what I could tell you. Them plots I sold, they're nothin', nothin' at all compared to...."

"To what?"

He squinted at me, pushing his tongue into his cheek and turning back his lower lip until it caressed his Adam's apple.

"Compared to what I *know*," he whispered. He cackled, an eerie sound against the silence of the cemetery, then leaned closer and winked. "Lord love...a duck!"

The duck was flying through the heavens—you know, the ones with Pearly Gates and St. Peter and all that. I mean, there it was, through a cleft in the smog—Heaven itself, guarded by flights of ducks and chickens. And this one duck winging down to me like death on feathers, a scroll tucked under its wing as it squawked a duckish version of "When the Saints Come Marching In." As it hit the smog bank, the clouds welded together and closed off Heaven.

But not before I have a chance to look at it—just one glance, and that a quick one, but it was enough.

I saw the Golden Streets, paved with pigs and sheep and geese and bunnies and frogs...arched marbled window casements with horned heads poking out and looking silly. That was it.

The angelic duck whooshed closer, circling my head and sliding down toward the tombstone. The old man sat there, cackling toothlessly—"A plot, a plot, your immortal soul for a plot"—and I began to get a glimmering.

Animals, you know, don't usually get buried. Or if they do, it is in some haphazard way, like in an old cigar box festooned with cast-off plasticized Christmas bows. Most of the time, it's a brief funeral in the bottom of a black Hefty bag or burial at sea in the toilet bowl. But mostly they lay outside, in the open.

It's us, us humans, who crate ourselves up in satin and wood and lead and concrete, then dump a ton or so of sod on top to keep us down. And there we lie.

And there we lie—to ourselves, mostly. Because I know. I saw it. The grave's our ending place because we choose to make it so. We're so smart, we've boxed ourselves out of heaven.

The last I saw of it, the duck was heading south, joining up with a flight passing overhead. The old man still cackled as I stumbled away. And when I followed the tarred edge of the highway this time, I tried not to notice the frogs scattered around like so many bad memories.

I *tried* not to notice them, anyway.

JURY OF HIS PEERS

Two weeks after the unexpected death of Dean Hardley had shocked and grieved the academic community, then faded in importance before the annual visit of the accreditation team, Professor Potter walked ceremoniously the five blocks from his campus laboratory to the center of town, turned right on Main, and stepped up the brick stairway toward the Police Department.

The officer on duty barely spared a glance for the tall, thin, grey-haired figure who rapped lightly on the information desk.

"Yes, sir," the officer said, not looking up from the form he was filling out. "How may I help you?"

"I wish to report a murder," Potter announced in a low voice.

"I wish to report a murder," he repeated ten minutes later to another—presumably senior—officer behind another desk somewhere in the deep recesses of the building.

"I wish to report a murder," he repeated for the final time to the chief detective as he entered the spartan office, squinting in the harsh glare of an overhead light bar. In one corner, he noted, a split-leaf philodendron—

really a rather nice *philodendron bipinnatifidum*—struggled valiantly to survive in what had to be a hostile environment.

"But there was no murder," the detective answered. "As you've been told, the autopsy revealed death from natural causes. There were no signs of a struggle or forced entry, or of anything except one aging, rather excitable man with a weak heart."

"Yes, I know," Potter said. "I followed the case quite closely in the media. I know exactly what was found. Exactly what I planned for you to find. But that does not alter the facts. I wish to report a murder."

The detective sighed. "All right, Mr. Potter...."

"*Professor* Potter, please."

"Professor Potter. All right, then, how did you murder Hardley?"

"Well, I didn't actually, although...."

"Hold on, you just admitted to a murder...."

"On the contrary, I merely reported that there *was* one. I did not kill Dean Hardley, not physically at least, although I suppose I am legally responsible. I know that I am morally responsible. They told me that."

"Okay, get on with it. How did you...what, *expedite...engineer*, is that a better word?...the murder."

"It was quite simple, actually. And I can *prove* that I did it. Tell me, did you men find a very small metallic cylinder attached to the headboard of Dean Hardley's bed when they searched the room? It was perhaps half-an-inch thick and about two inches long. It would look very like a spent cartridge, in fact."

The detective studied the typed report on his desk. His forefinger followed a ling of print down one page, halfway down a second. Then two rather surprised blue eyes glanced up over the rims of a pair of glasses.

"Yes, they did. The lab tested it but there wasn't anything suspicious about it, other than its location."

"Not by then. The gas dissipates rapidly when exposed to normal atmosphere. By the next morning there would have been no trace."

"Gas?"

"Yes, a derivative of the African.... Oh dear, this will be rather complicated. May I speak in simplified terms?"

"By all means, Mr., er..., Professor Potter. Please do."

"Well, for many years I have engage in research in plant physiology. Body structures, if you will. My laboratory at the university is unusually well stocked with rare and exotic specimens, including one which, when properly prepared, can be transformed into a remarkably effective tranquilizing gas. The gas is odorless, colorless, leaves no residue, and, under certain conditions, is completely harmless. It merely relaxes the body's muscles, bringing on uninterrupted rest."

Potter paused for a moment to adjust his thick spectacles.

"Under other circumstances, however, the gas is somewhat more potent. It still relaxes, but does so completely. The heart, the lung muscles, in fact all of the major muscles of the body slow down at first, then begin to miss their natural rhythms, and finally simply stop. Death is very quick and entirely painless.

"Dean Hardley simply went to sleep when the gas was released in his bedroom, quite near his head."

"And you did this? How did you get in to administer the gas."

"Well, in a manner of speaking, I did…and I didn't. I placed the cylinder—during what was supposed to be a short visit to the bathroom when I visited one day—after assuring myself that Audr…"—he swallowed hard, trying not to remember Audra's look of joy as she received his engagement ring so many years before—"that Mrs. Hardley was out of town and in no danger. She is totally innocent, of course. I wanted only to…to remove the Dean. But I did not…I… that is, I didn't actually *activate* the cylinder. Some…my accomplice did that. And that is why they insisted that I confess."

Potter looked down at his fingernails and sighed deeply.

"Your accomplice?" The detective fiddled impatiently with a pen set on his desk.

"Yes, a.…. This is rather complicated again." Potter stood and crossed the room, standing next to the *philodendron bipinnatifidum*. He fingered the veins of a large, faintly brown-edged leaf.

"You know, you really shouldn't have this plant here alone, like this. To grow properly, plants must have the proper light and humidity, and the proximity of other.…"

"Professor," the detective said softly.

"Ah, yes. Sorry." He stood there silently, then dropped his hand. "Are you familiar with the name of Cleve Backster?"

The detective thought for a second or two before answering. "No."

"I thought not. About fifty years ago, Backster discovered that many plants have systems analogous to the human nervous system. The do, in fact, feel, react, and respond to emotions, to various stimuli, to danger.

"You mean like when people sing to their house-plants, play classical music, that sort of thing?"

"Well, infinitely more sophisticated, of course, but yes, that sort of thing."

"And here I always though my wife was crazy," the detective said *sotto voce*. Potter did not appear to have heard.

"In many plants," Potter continued without interruption, "these systems are quite well developed. In one remarkable early experiment, another scientist, Paul Sauvin, actually started an automobile engine by sending a strong emotional telepathic message to a houseplant over two miles away. The plant in turned triggered a radio signal that actually turned on the ignition.

"In effect, a philodendron started the car."

The detective stared, comprehension and incredulity battling on his face. Potter continued as if unaware of his listener.

"Three months or so ago, I isolated and identified a

number of electrical responses to external stimuli in plants. I worked through several strains before deciding on precisely the proper plant—a common dracaena, by the way, *dracaena sanderiana*. I established a strong empathetic bond between myself and the plant...and trained it to listen to me, if you wish, until I could initiate a response merely by directing any strongly emotional thoughts to the plant.

"That was the first step.

"The next step was more difficult. I constructed a cylinder—the one your men found—capping it with a radio-sensitive plate that snapped off when exposed to a specific stimulus. And I hid the cylinder in Dean Hardley's room during my supposed bathroom visit.

"That evening, I had presented him with a gift, a dracaena suitably potted in a silver container that was part planter, part signal amplifier. Later, when I arrived home and felt certain that Dean Hardley would be in bed—he was notoriously regular in his habits, you know, and that made everything easier—I...I triggered the stimulus."

"You mean...," the detective began.

"Yes. In reality, the dracaena killed Dean Hardley. I.... I...." Potter shuddered, as if unable to continue. He screwed his eyes shut and concentrated on the memory of the bruises on Audra's arms, the look of desperation he had begun seeing in her eyes lately. "I could not count on a mere emotional transmission on my part, not over the twelve miles from my apartment to Dean Hardley's home, so I augmented my own thoughts with another signal. I...I threatened the plant. I threatened to burn it, and actually did burn a leaf from one of its sister plants."

The detective stared, his hands stilled and motionless on the desk blotter.

"The dracaena reacted instantly and violently. The silver pot amplified the transmission, and the amplified signal shattered the seal on the cylinder. Dean Hardley died within minutes, unaware that he was breathing death even as he slept. He was dead when Mrs. Hardley returned home from visiting their children the next day."

Potter dropped his hand to his side and returned to his chair. When he sat down, he slumped.

The detective leaned forward and punched a button on his intercom.

"Jennings," he ordered, "send someone over to the Hardley house and ask Mrs. Hardley if there is a... what did you call it?"

This last was directed to Potter.

"A dracaena. A 'lucky bamboo' plant."

"A bamboo-like plant," the detective continued. "A house plant, in a silver pot."

"It was in the living room," Potter added, helpfully.

"Probably in the living room. If there is one, get it over here, pronto."

The detective leaned back.

"Tell me, Professor, why did you come in here today? In the two weeks since the death...."

"The murder."

"All right, since the murder, there hasn't been even the slightest suspicion of anything other than a natural death. Your name has not even been mentioned. Certainly no one has suggested so exotic a murder scheme. So why did you come here today, to confess to what sounds as if it might be a perfect crime?"

Potter stared at his fingers again, long thin fingers, sensitive and smooth.

"You won't find the plant at Audr…at Mrs. Hardley's," he said, as if unaware of the detective's question. "The pot may still be there, but the dracaena is dead."

The detective did not speak but his eyebrows arched in an unstated question. Potter stood again, but this time he moved slowly toward the side of the room farthest from the philodendron.

"You see, it knew what I had done. When I threatened it with fire, the plant had no alternative but to react; the systems are instinctive and automatic. Yet it was not wholly insensitive. It was in a room yards away from the gas, but as the cells in Hardley's body suffocated, they set up a resonating signal that the plant, already attuned to my own emotional states, intercepted. It realized, somehow, not with a brain or anything that complex, but on an instinctual level, that it had killed. It chose to die also.

"And as it died, it transmitted its own signal. They picked it up. I felt within a few days that they knew.

"*They*?" the detective asked, shaking his head. "Who? Your colleagues at the university?"

"No," Potter said, his head down cast but his hand

pointing steadily toward the philodendron. Already the leaf he had touched earlier was wilting, the brown edge biting deeper into the healthy structure of the leaf. "No. My plants. You see, I had always treated them with extreme care, and they flourished. But now they cannot trust me. I betrayed them. I tricked them into helping me destroy a life, and they have withdrawn from me. All plants.

"And plants are my life.

"Somehow, I felt that if I confessed, if I made what amends I could—even though I *still* believe that Dean Hardley deserved to be removed—I could...well, they might forgive me."

The detective remained quiet.

"I *had* to," Potter burst out, tears forming in his pale eyes. "How else could I ever look at them again, touch them again, without feeling their judgment. It was the only thing I could do."

Across the room, the wilted philodendron leaf already looked fresher, more alive.

ABOUT THE AUTHOR

MICHAEL R. COLLINGS is an Emeritus Professor of English at Pepperdine University and the author of over thirty volumes of poetry, novels, short fiction, bibliography, literary criticism, and studies of writers including Stephen King, Dean R. Koontz, Piers Anthony, Brian W. Aldiss, and Orson Scott Card. Many of his books have been published by the Borgo Press Imprint of Wildside Press. In addition to *Wordsmith, Part One—The Veil of Heaven; Wordsmith, Part Two—The Thousand Eyes of Flame;* and *Three Tales of Omne,* he has published two novels, *Singer of Lies* (science-fiction) and *The House Beyond the Hill* (horror). He and his wife now live in southwestern Idaho.